CAT LOVER

Dan Spencer is a prize-winning author whose prose poems and flash fictions regularly appear in journals including *Popshot*, *Litro*, *Gutter* and *New Writing Scotland*, among other places. He grew up in a commuter town outside London and earned a bachelor's in English Literature with Creative Writing from UEA and a master's in Creative Writing at the University of Glasgow. He's also a teacher of international students and has worked in Osaka and Riyadh. Right this moment, you'll find him by the sea near Newcastle, with a wife, two lovely daughter~~~ ~~~ two lovely cats.

CW01496567

CAT LOVER

Dan Spencer

Atlantic Books
London

Published in trade paperback in Great Britain in 2024 by
Atlantic Books, an imprint of Atlantic Books Ltd.

This paperback edition published in 2026 by Atlantic Books.

10 9 8 7 6 5 4 3 2 1

A CIP catalogue record for this book is available from the British Library.

Paperback ISBN: 978 180546 171 5
E-book ISBN: 978 1 80546 170 8

Printed and bound by CPI (UK) Ltd, Croydon CR0 4YY

Atlantic Books
An imprint of Atlantic Books Ltd
Ormond House
26–27 Boswell Street
London
WC1N 3JZ

www.atlantic-books.co.uk

Product safety EU representative: Authorised Rep Compliance Ltd., Ground Floor,
71 Lower Baggot Street, Dublin, D02 P593, Ireland. www.arccompliance.com

To B.

'We'd better open the door and see.'

Judith Kerr

1.

'Goodbye, cat! Goodbye, flat!'

The door closes: he wakes and he's Berry. He stretches, pushing parts of Berry away from other parts of Berry. Getting onto the floor, he goes through the rooms, doorway to hallway, hallway to doorway, room to room. Lamps left lit, here and there. Ghostly colours, soaking out of everything.

He's waiting for something. Checking. Auditing. A place for everything. It's a jigsaw. And Berry's a moving piece of the puzzle, going through the rooms, searching, seeking, waiting. 'When... when?' says the thought, twitching like a bit of thread you pat at with your paw. He gives it voice but it goes nowhere, a small keening sound, appearing in the air, dissolving...

The kitchen. He makes a fluid, S-shaped movement, a slosh of water, and he's up onto the counter. He's leapt like this before, knows it all. The grip of grout between the tiles. Sleek side of the cupboard. Clip-clopping kitchen-top pots. Stop, at the window. Wait.

Listen. Listen to the noises of the building. Piano. Voices. Floorboards. Shouting. A slammed door. You hear this in houses sometimes: raised voices which fade away again, forgotten. *That's where you are, Berry, in a building, in a flat, what you are, Berry, a cat in a flat...*

He waits. He knows he's waiting, but what's he waiting for? 'Ivy,' says the voice inside his head. It's Ivy. And he's Berry. He's alive inside Berry. Lithe and alive inside Berry. But how long has it been?

Outside is the garden. The high garden wall. Steps leading up to the gate through which, any moment now, she'll appear. *Ivy.* Last light's long left the lawn. But you still see sunshine in the tops of the high, bare cherry trees in the park beyond the wall.

In the window now he sees Berry's face, reflected, the garden dark. Didn't notice the day changing. Didn't *not* notice. *How long has it been? Have you slept again, Berry?* Not easy to say. He can't simply say, 'I'm awake now,' or, 'Now I'm sleeping,' or, 'Now I'm in a dream.'

In the black window's reflection, the shining face covered in black fur. Two beings, Berry and him, watching each other. *Stay wary. Know where you stand. What's Berry. What's you. What's not...* It looks hollow, the face of the cat. Spooky like an owl. Where's Ivy? Why hasn't she come?

Coming and going at strange times, sleeping and waking in the day and night, hard to hold on to her, the idea of her, but soon she'll appear in the dark in the gate in the wall then on the steps into the garden then on the path through the garden then entering through the door into the kitchen, pushing her feet from her shoes and crossing the cold kitchen to enter the hallway, to sit on the floor in the hallway...

... and he'll go to her, instinctively and wilfully, offering her Berry's head, and she'll hold it in her hand, his head in her hand, warm little skull, rubbing it in her hand, his head fitting her hand, her hand fitting his head, ball-and-socket, and those small growling sounds of their happiness rising from somewhere within them, between them, around them.

2.

She's reached a place where she can do it without think-ing. Ten years ago, she needed the clinical checklists; those tick-box procedures (borrowed from the pre-flight checks of airline pilots), they were literal lifesavers. In fact, at first, they hadn't helped her like they should have done. More often, they were a series of turnstiles, block-ing her and blocking her. She couldn't keep them tidy in her head, all those ticks falling like pins.

But these days her head doesn't come into it. You learn it in your body. Your mind is in your body. Your hands know how to work. Your voice knows what to say. Some days, she's so outside herself, she doesn't think a single worded thought. The name 'Ivy' never occurs to her. That's the goal, that's the want: not to think, not to think about it.

There are difficult days, of course, but Ivy isn't there, only the goodness of her knowledge and abilities. There are days like today, at the Southern Royal, when a child is lost, one you couldn't hold out hope for. A young man really, not a child. But he didn't know he was a man yet, didn't talk like one, didn't move like one. He'd been larking about like a child. He'd fallen like a child. There'd been no saving him. The mother called to him. He didn't answer. Brain death. The lungs breathed, the heart beat. The body lay closed like a door.

Each time it happens, you pause to pay attention to yourself. Are you here? *Check*. Are you now? *Check*. Do you feel it? How much do you feel it? Days like today, you go back over everything, ensuring that procedures were followed. Checking. Auditing. It's required. It's only right. You can disappear into here. You can disappear into now.

When doctors lose a child, there are parents who say that you did all you could and others who say, 'What went wrong? What didn't you do?' And there are parents, like today, only the mother alone this time, who are both people at once, who say everything, back and forth, and all over the place, thanking you and blaming you and crying out in all sorts of ways.

Days like today, if Clover phones to say, 'How was work?', Ivy will answer immediately, 'We had a death,' and she'll feel her sister, inside the phone, recoil.

She should be gentler with Clover. It's too cold, too sudden of a plunge into Ivy's world, to be told it like that. *A death, another death!* Like dinner being served: Voilà!

But if Clover doesn't want to know the answer, she still wants to ask. Ivy knows what she's up to. Clover's feeling out her sister's sorrow. *How's your colour? How's your temperature? Can you describe the pain? Is it sharp or more of an ache?* Clover's running through her own series of checks, whenever Clover calls.

Of course, what follows the lost child is unrelated. They lost the child in the day. They spent the day losing the child. The Head Wound arrives much later.

When he comes, Ivy's shift is long finished but the hospital has flowed on, carrying her with it.

It's very early or very late. They're in those six months called winter. Signs of morning look a long way off. Up here, in this country, this time of year, it can be night-time all day. But she's happy with the dark. It's something good about this season. Whatever your shift, night or day, you can enter in darkness, leave in darkness.

When the Head Wound turns up, Ivy is standing drinking tea. She's made tea for the nurses. Back home, an empty flat awaits. But there's company here. She's made tea, an actual brewed pot, signifying something. A much-needed message to the nurses: *We're in this together. I'm with you in this.* As a doctor, you have to get along with them. Really, you're alone in it, but there's this message she's speaking. *Come, drink tea. Come, talk with me.*

6

'Sad,' the nurse is saying. 'Terrible. Dreadful. I know, I know. I don't know how you do it, Doctor Dover. Just a lad. The poor boy. His poor mother. That poor dead boy. Just a fall. Just a game. Just boys being boys. Only one misstep and that's it. How do you do it? Stay so professional. So untouched? So clinical?' The nurse pauses, takes a sip, lets her compliment sink in.

No, it is very sad, says Ivy.

'And you with your losses, Doctor Dover.'

Yes, we do all have losses, don't we. But you can't make it personal.

'But you,' says the nurse. 'With *your* losses. Close to home.'

Ivy has nothing to add. Why discuss Iain Keele with this woman? Would this woman even know about that? Ivy simply smiles, sips, moves her head a little.

'And then the investigations, the paperwork!' says the nurse. 'They always think there's negligence, don't they? The loved ones. They always think the doctor did something wrong, when we all know you didn't, because you didn't, did you? You can't have done—? What could you have done differently? You probably wonder about that.'

No, nothing to be done.

'Not that we haven't seen some mistakes in our time. The eyes and ears, us nurses. Almost invisible, we are. But the things you see! The things some doctors do! Then lowly yours-truly has to pipe up, "Excuse me, Doctor, are you sure that's the right dosage?"'

That's nurses for you. Full of respect and admiration but always ready with their tuts and told-you-sos. The heart and soul and muscle of the profession but then they have to be the brains as well.

'What gets me through,' says the nurse, 'is my man. Someone to talk to. Someone to complain to. Not that he listens, but it does the job.'

For me it's the cat, says Ivy.

It's half a joke. A pet cat can't be compared to a human partner. Everyone knows it. But now Ivy is saying how undeniably lovely, how loving Berry is, how he'll come seeking her when she's most vulnerable, like a kitten, like a child, nuzzling her still fingers, climbing her resting legs, patting his paws at her dreaming face, calling out sweet nothings, unendingly.

'Aye,' says the nurse. 'Devious wee bastards, aren't they?'

It's then that someone looks in on them, seeking another pair of hands. The backlog is burgeoning. Could somebody jump in and clear a few patients? This fellow, this head wound, perhaps?

The nurse doesn't turn around but holds her mug tight, squeezing the last of its warmth, taking her time, contemplating something. 'A cat's not a man, though, of course,' she says. 'Do you have that, Doctor Dover? A man. Someone. Have you found that again?'

Then Ivy looks past her and answers that she'll see to him, the Head Wound.

A head wound isn't unusual at this time of night. She thinks nothing of it. And seamstress work isn't really in her job description, plus the nurses are proprietorial about it, but tonight the staff's diminished (when isn't it?) and everyone has their hands full, so Ivy stitches him up as a last task, like she's tying a bow on the end of the day.

He's a big man, the Head Wound. She sits him in a chair, pulls the curtain half across. *I feel like a tree surgeon!* she thinks, orienting herself around him. His knots, his whorls. He has the odours of the woods, the streets, the cold outside. Fumes lift off him like an idling truck.

Let's take a look at you.

As she gently brushes at his brow, as she leans over him, the man tries to explain himself: 'Football,' he offers, and she can't help but say, Football? What kind of match ends in this?

The other, American kind of football, it turns out, though he doesn't seem to be from there, does he? Where's that accent from? She can't place it.

'A friendly,' he says. 'Shirts and skins. I know what you're thinking. Not very friendly, eh? Or you're thinking how it's not the season—?'

No, she wasn't thinking anything. But now she sees a gang of men bashing skulls on a floodlit field. Shirts

9

and skins. Darkness. Pools of light. Men. Unbidden, she imagines the span of his bare shoulders, perspiration on his neck, his thick back, heavy breathing… But why, when she feels no desire for him whatsoever?

Sorry.

He has flinched. She wasn't being careful. Is he tender? Wasn't she tender enough? Did she assume, as she pulled the suture, that he wouldn't feel the pinch, a strongman like this?

For some time, she says nothing more. *Focus on the job in hand. The head in hand.* To treat this small amount of damage, there's no need to ask more questions, to do more digging.

Already, she has him figured out, hasn't she? She's used to men like this, with these late-night injuries. You can guess what they get up to. The bad choices of men at night. What's different is he's cleaned himself up. He's put on a fresh shirt. On the collar, a little blood has dripped. His hair is still wet from the shower, the skin flushed. A slight breath of alcohol lifts from his pores.

She watches her own hands as they care for the head.

A weighty, lumpy object. There's lots to it, much to discover. The brow protrudes and seems to separate into two fists. The forehead is marked and rough. At the hairline, where the hair grows wildly (like gorse), the scalp becomes smooth and round. The nose has a strong bridge then it's bulbous at the end. Under the eyes, the skin sags but the face, as a whole, is fleshy. Much of him is hidden under that beard. An endlessly intriguing case. A terrain her fingers navigate...

... and she's travelling back ten years or more to that first head, the old woman, the head she shared with three other students, that first week of medical school, whole bodies too hard to come by. Tonight, her mind keeps travelling out. She keeps leaving herself. It's not like her. She isn't like herself...

Impossible, at first, the head on the table. The head of the bodiless woman. So still. So pale. Its death, its beauty. Impossible to reach out to it. To touch it... And she's thinking of Keele again, of holding Keele's head. Keele's head in her hands. Keele's hard and angular head. Keele's spiky mind. The dart of Keele's eyes. Keele's lips flickering as he talks and talks, only ever shut up with a kiss...

'You're good at that,' says the Head Wound.

He's looking up at her. He has these boyish, baggy eyes he's gazing up at her with. Watery moons in pink hammocks. He's watching her hands, or trying to, peering up through his eyebrows. Her hands. His head. They're things outside of them, beyond them.

Keep your scalp still, please.

'You could do it in your sleep, I bet,' he continues, with a winking voice, and his meaning must be, mustn't it, to call to mind her bedroom. It's what he's up to. She knows him – not him, but men like him, talk like this. The sly flattery of the night-time arrivals. The men who call you 'nurse' to wrongfoot you, then sweep you off your feet.

Then, momentarily, it occurs to her she likes him – not him, but men like him; not likes them, but likes the easiness of them, their straightforwardness, their obviousness, their simplicity. You know exactly what they are, what they want, every move they make. She laughs and he probably thinks he's done it, lured her somehow. No chance!

She's finished with him. But she's so deep now into another work schedule that she might as well stay on. It wouldn't be her first back-to-back double. She might as well stay until sunrise, a different woman on a different timeline.

Then, as she sees off the Head Wound, she hears herself saying, Listen, shall we get a drink?

I'll drive. Parked over here. Unlocked now. You can get in.

His side leans like a rowboat as he clambers down into the passenger seat. His feet push aside the half-empty water bottles in the footwell.

She reverses out, travels down the ramps, follows the route for the exit. The hospital is quiet, its lights very still. The hospital gives nothing away, doesn't seem to clock them, doctor and patient, leaving together. They take the tunnel under the river. They watch the road. They keep finding nothing to say.

'Where's open at this time of night?' wonders the Head Wound. 'Everywhere's always closing early. We're not continental round here.'

Not anymore, she says.

Standing outside in the cold, sandstone city, they queue for Fair Isle (that deconsecrated church with a late licence) alongside other turnouts hoping to be stayouts. The bouncer at the door checks them over like a first aider. Inside there's a lot of noise, but Ivy wants noise. *Let me not hear myself think*: a prayer. Everyone inside is worse for wear. But it's beautiful, in the wee hours, slipping into a vestry with a stranger and a whisky.

In their alcove, there's nowhere to sit. He disappears and comes back with a stool – 'Pull up a pew' – then stands around her like a bodyguard. On the wall, backlit, is a futuristic, stained-glass picture of Adam and Eve. She blinks at the neon. What's he saying? Something about planets or plates? Is he an astronomer? An astrologer?

She's laughing, easily tickled, in the small hours. It's ridiculous, being with a man like this. Just look at him! Just listen!

'Thousands and thousands of years,' he's saying, and whatever it is, it's amusing, with this large, tall, big, fat man and this talk of long, long, human-less time sweeping her forward. Then it's not funny but wonderful and what is it? Is she empty? Is she finally empty? Or was she empty before? This evening with him, what is it, this feeling? Is she finally emptying out? Or finally filling again? And where is she? In a bar with this man, but it feels like she's floating, flowing. What's he saying now? *Ages and ages of ages and ages for ages and ages...*

It isn't him. No, it isn't him. He's nobody. It isn't because of him. And it isn't during the last drink. That's not when she decides to sleep with him. It isn't once they're outside, wobbling down the road. She'd decided already. She'd decided before she drank anything. She'd decided before saying 'Let's get a drink', before treating his head, before saying a word to him or even setting eyes on him.

It's nothing to do with him. It's that something has ended today. It was hours before. When something ended. When something began. It was when they lost the child. It was when she knew they would lose the child. That's when she chose to invite someone, anyone, home to her bed.

3.

The screech of a fox: he's awake. And already hiding under the armchair. Night. Dark colours in the room. Orange light in the window. The fox-cry dwindles. Gone. Retreated. But somewhere out there still, the predator, gone into those ranks and ranks of urban bushes.

Berry creeps forward.

So, you're afraid of foxes? comes the thought. But whose fear is it? From where inside him did it rear up? Where in Berry did he feel it? Where did he think it?

He enters the hallway.

The black hallway. Something's in the hallway. Her door, in the hallway, never closed, is closed. He pushes. Cheek, neck, the side of his body, a leaning motion, he pushes at the door but it won't open. He speaks. It won't open. Something's here.

Behind him, it stands in the kitchen doorway. Something. Freeze. Don't look at it. God, it's huge! Don't look right at it, don't move, don't think. Listen. Listen to yourself, to your instincts, to Berry's instincts. Look for escapes. Look for shadows.

It's too large, the body. A large, deep area of gloom. Filling the kitchen doorway. An intruder, seeming to climb through the doorway. Seeming to climb through a window into their den. A mass of gloom and, in that mass, body parts. Weighty, born-down shoulders. Big thighs. A copious beard. The lean of its erection under a stomach broad and fat and hard. The air swimming with darkness and cold…

But heat comes off the body. Too much to stand. Its smell, its temperature, its pull, the pulse of it… and 'No' is the thought, 'No' is the feeling, no, no, no… like it's come, like you knew it would come, knew it would one day come, to take her from you, to take her, to take…

A big hand lifts to an invisible face. A bright glass, resting springily against the beard. Unbearable. It's drinking. Water trickles. Slowly. Water trickling through the giant, living thing. Water trickling in its throat, into its organs, like a spring through rock…

Knock goes the glass on the kitchen table. Then it's turned back again. The arm bearing out. Opening the door, her door. Quick, dart! Slip inside. Snake in and out of his stride. Inside, into her room, and she's there!

Ivy.

It's her. Repositioning her body. Too real. Lit too starkly by the headboard clamp-lamp. Ivy. Re-articulating. Lengthening. Lying differently, so that maybe, really, is it even really her?

'Hello again,' she says.

It casts a spell.

It breaks a spell.

Then the man lowers down. The readied man. Limb by limb, felling himself. The bed giving way. The whole room giving way around him. Lake-waves spreading through the walls, the windows... Suddenly lit up, there's his face. The thing's face. Too large, like every part of him. Taped to the forehead, a white pad. A red cut shows at the eyebrow, at the hairline. He has her. Is she pulling away?

'Hello?' she says again, uncertain.

Like a voice answering an unknown number.

Not right. None of this. They aren't right. Willowy Ivy. And this hulk. This bull and this willow tree. Can't be. Mustn't be. Not what she wants.

But she sweeps Berry away, keeps sweeping him away. Again, he gets onto the bed, and she sweeps him away with the wing of her arm. Unseeing. Seeing only the man, who absorbs everything. This overbearing man, weighing on her. Or seeing nothing. Not him. Not herself. Trying not to see. Getting somewhere else. Getting elsewhere. Going and going and gone and going...

No one hears Berry. Nothing comes out as words. Does he even exist? It's truly horrible. At the worst moment, she's on her shins, curled over herself, the man crouching too, encasing her, the woman you love curled up like an ammonite inside this monster.

4.

In the morning, she's alone. He's gone. Did he sleep there? And did Ivy really just drift off afterwards, with that huge man next to her?

It's early. She lies there, diagnosing the light in the room. The nightshift ahead of her is far-off on the horizon. Soon enough she'll be back at the hospital – *the scene of the crime!* – but until then there's a day to be filled somehow. How to fill it?

The thought comes again: *Am I empty? Am I full?*

She notices then that Berry isn't on the bed for once, isn't right on top of her for once, her personal alarm clock. So, she gets up and goes looking for him. He must be in hiding for some reason, because he doesn't come running at her footsteps or her calls, not until she gets his breakfast. That draws him out. *Is that all you're about, my boy?*

While the cat eats, she sits with him, thinking about last night, seeing herself in that situation, trying it on for size.

Goodness me, Ivy. Did you really…?

She laughs like it's a life taken lightly. But it's not the right pose.

Then: *What was I doing? Being with him. Not like me. He wasn't like him. Not like Keele. He wasn't anything like him. What was I doing? You can't go opening your door to any waif or stray. Just to see what happens… No, I don't like men like him. He's not like I'm like. Keele, I liked. I was his. I'm still his…* Is she speaking or thinking? Living on her own, she sometimes can't tell.

God… the thought of it… She and that man last night…

What a pair! she says.

She's glad he's gone.

Just me, cat, she says.

She's completely alone.

Another thought: *What would Clover say?*

Once before, not long after Keele, Ivy tried meeting someone. In a booth, in a bar, she and this man had kissed incessantly for an hour, until their mouths hurt. Neither one had mentioned sex. Neither had thought of the other that way. So, what were they doing? She'd giggled a lot about it afterwards on the phone to Clover.

'I think it's healthy,' Clover had said, weighing her responses before offering them. 'I do, now I think about it. Yes, that's it, Sis! The best medicine. Back on the horse!'

The horse? Was Clover a vet, in that scenario? Had Ivy ever done much horse-riding?

'Yes, healthy,' Clover had said. 'Healthy and helpful, whether it leads to anything or not. But, now we mention it, would you like it to lead somewhere?'

What, then, about this man last night? The impracticably big man. The badly injured man. What would Clover say about him? Healthy and helpful? No, it was confused. Unsophisticated. She doesn't want that want. Anyway, it's over now. It's nothing to do with her anymore. She doesn't want that man, or to think about his body…

A good shower, that levels her out. The cubicle is like another room. Stepping back into the bathroom, in a mist, she could be a different person. No, she won't again be so foolishly wide awake as she was with the man last night. There's no question, she won't see him again. Above the sink, the photograph of Keele is steamed over.

Next, she takes herself out to the flowers and vegetables shop, The Cutting, to buy a mediumly roasted coffee and a lightly sparkling lemonade.

As she enters the shop, the neighbour from One-Two is leaving, her arm crooking a wicker basket. Bread in a brown paper bag. The elaborate green tassels of seven thin carrots.

The shopkeeper's doorbell rings in their Sunday.

Bonnie morning, Ivy says.

One-Two winces at that. 'You needn't trot out dialect for my sake, Ivy. Rather unconvincing. I myself was born and bred here but am never one for patois.'

Lovely morning.

'Yes, lovely,' says One-Two. 'Always a lovely morning in our lovely local grocer. Nice they know your name. Our names. Whenever one collects one's orders. How it used to be. How it could be. A village in the city.'

We're lucky.

'Luck's nothing to do with it. You get what you pay for, after all. Lovely mornings like this. Bought and paid for. Not a lovely night, though. All the caterwauling.'

Foxes? Cats?

'Among others, yes… The Youths,' she says, like it's a proper noun. 'The Young. But it is a lovely morning, I agree, for the most part. A lovely morning, whilst the youthful and the drunk are still sleeping it off.'

Well, goodbye.

Back to the flat. Back by the back door, the back way, on the back lane. How she always comes and goes, hoping to happen upon no one. It jarred, meeting One-Two in the doorway. It got her thinking about people again; about neighbours, homeowners, roommates, lodgers, the man last night… She lives in a neighbourhood filled with people… But she does love her home, doesn't she? In this tall, terraced tenement house. On its long, wandering street of tall, bright tenements…

At the gate, she looks down the steps into the sunken garden. The way they built it, a hundred and fifty years ago, her flat opens onto the garden at the back, but at the front her home is halfway underground. From the street, steps descend to her front door. Little light gets in. And from the street, too, other steps lead up to the main entrance, the broad door into that capacious, red stairwell onto which the apartments of all those worthies open… steps she rarely has a need to climb.

Some days she thinks the building is a doll's house. Double-fronted, you could swing open its walls like a cupboard and discover a cross-section of all their lives going on inside. Her home is Minus One-One, then above it is Zero-One, then One-One, then Two-One. And on the other side of the tenement there is Cox-Coburn – Mr Duplex – who has his own grand private entrance and whose home encompasses both the basement level and the ground floor. Above him is One-Two then Two-Two.

Other days, Ivy thinks the building is a ship. She's in the lower decks, the third-class cabins, while above her they dine at the captain's table. Above her, they captain. In this listed building. In this building listing like a ship.

And she thinks of the neighbours as mothers and fathers, uncles and aunts, though not one single resident, in fact, has a child. You couldn't imagine a child running wild in these flats, on these stairs, in this garden. You can't imagine what the neighbours would make of it, those shouts and running footsteps in this quiet, in this calm. But Ivy often feels like a child around them, no matter how old she gets, how experienced, how much she experiences.

Anyway, she's glad she's through another interaction with One-Two, that lonely, nosy woman, that woman taking in lodgers... But it must have looked friendly enough – their morning interaction – successful enough. Let them be, and they'll let Ivy be. She can do it. She's been good at it – until recently. She's been able to keep herself running quietly here, without incident, without interruption.

She remembers the day she moved in, eighteen years old, her first year studying at the university... and One-Two had welcomed her in the garden, coolly saying, 'Well, up until now, we've been able to price out the students, thank goodness...'

What a hateful woman! One-Two: conducting her hate through her pleasantries... Hateful, that's the truth. Takes one to know one.

Back in the flat, the cat has disappeared again. Coming into the kitchen, at her garden door, Ivy calls, but it's in hiding. Funny animal. Ivy stands by the sink and drinks her coffee down and then, more slowly, the lemonade.

You can fix yourself up. You can sit yourself down. You can run a consultation inside your own head. *The doctor will see you now. You can go right in...* View it objectively. Assess what symptoms you can. Prescribe the necessary meal or chore. And where no cure presents itself, let it go. Where no obvious course of treatment occurs, let it go. Pick yourself up. Move on. Having no solution is like having no problem at all.

Finally, she finds him, the cat, in one of his places. Under the armchair. She drags him out and puts him on her lap. Like she's passing fingers through her own hair, she runs a hand over him, one single stroke, head to tail-tip. But the animal twitches and runs away again. *Nervy thing! Did I do something wrong? What's eating it? If only humans had it so simple...*

Something's sticky on Ivy's thumb. *Getting into messes again, Berry? Been in the bins?* Or is it Ivy's stickiness? *Seep, leak, ooze, flood...* she thinks horrible words, thinks horrible thoughts, thinks of bodies. Sometimes even the cat's body is too much; even her own... A mistake, the man's body last night. A mistake, going with him...

What makes it worse, she was cruel. Last night. She'd laughed in his face! He'd taken it on the chin, but when she'd guffawed at what he said about being an astrologer or astronomer, what was she being if not cruel? *You heard the word 'astronomy' and the idea that this hulking bloke held a doctorate amused you, you shit, you shitty woman...*

It turned out he was speaking about 'geology'. Still, he was an academic. He was working at the university, chiselling and polishing a hefty thesis. But she hadn't seen that. When they'd met, she'd seen him as just another head-wound headcase.

Even now, she still can't shake the idea she's better than him, that she was allowing him her presence.

He's proud. He reckons he's done well for himself, getting me, she was thinking all night. *He's proud,* she was thinking, as this geologist bought her a drink, or placed his big body close to hers, or left the bar by her side. She'd never felt prized quite like that before. She'd never before felt like a precious stone. Cold, yes, and hard, but not precious.

That whole night with the Geologist... Outside Fair Isle, walking home, she'd gone on teasing him. Across the street, the botanic gardens had been black and silent behind their railings. The plants had lain like a sleeping zoo. They'd turned, the two of them, away from the iron gates and down the high street, south towards the river...

Last night, last night, last night... a delicious quiet had lasted, all along the dreaming high street, but broken here and there by yelps from other paired-up drunks. That night, that unreal night... she'd felt sober, in her drunkenness. She'd felt clear-sighted. Again and again they were about to part ways. And that would have been the end of it. But every turn she took, he took it too.

Are you lost?

'No,' he said.

He looked at her oddly.

'No, I know my way home.'

Me too, she said, frowning at him.

And he frowned too. A smiling frown. A frowning smile.

It was becoming a little worrisome.

You're not stalking me, are you?

She'd said it to make it funny, to make it untrue. But it didn't help. With new fear, she noticed again the wound on his head. She began to speak, her lips a small O, forming a word like *who* or *where* or *what*…

He shrugged. Then: 'I know where you live!' – growling, grinning, waggling his fingers.

Stop, I'm not joking!

She was suddenly looking around her, checking her surroundings. The side of the church. The backs of tenements. The trees. The row of restaurant bins. They were passing through Cherry Park. On the climbing frame, in the darkness, two teenagers huddled around a glowing phone. The boy was trying it on with the girl. The shrubbery and shadows, they brimmed with foxes and teenagers.

'Sorry,' the Geologist said.

He seemed cautious. He leaned away from her.

'Sorry, I got it wrong,' he said. 'Think I misread something. Thought you were joking too. Thought we were both… weren't we playing?' Now it was he who looked nervous, worried. She saw the small boy in him.

'But of course I know where you live,' he said. 'We live in the same building… Hold on, you do know that, don't you?' He'd taken a few steps away from her, staring at her with bemusement or concern. 'You did know who I was? We say hi sometimes. Didn't you recognize me at the hospital?'

And she had to backtrack. She had to keep going.

No, absolutely I did. Absolutely I knew you.

Suddenly, she really did feel drunk. She kept tripping up. He kept tripping her up. But her mistakes only made her more suspicious of him.

She pretended to be funny.

No, of course, I was joking too.

She laughed loudly like a teenager. A fox-like bark.

I know it's you, she said. You're the flatmate in Two-One.

If he was angry, he gave nothing away.

'The lodger in One-Two,' he said.

They'd reached the lane.

They were through that dark, triangular cherry tree park. They were nearly home. Her home. His home. Over the wall, she looked down on her garden. The lawn was a murky, black pond.

The Geologist might have been lying somehow. If she didn't recognize him, wasn't it because they'd never met? He wanted her, didn't he? Wasn't that what this was about? But what was it he wanted with her? What if he wanted her hurt and dead in a back lane like this one? And how, really, had he injured that forehead?

Did she have the guts to call him out on it? *You're lying! We've never met! Just try it! I'll scream the whole street awake!* She could have said it. So what if he was a good man? So what if it bruised his feelings? Anyone can be a good boy and a murderous beast at the same time. *Ivy, you're living too riskily tonight. Ivy, I don't know you at all.* It was time to put a halt to this.

She stood her ground. She wouldn't be intimidated. She put her neck out. She kissed him. The gate shook when he fell back against it. The size of him! The size of him, but she could bring him down!

Back in Cherry Park the teenage girl shouted at the teenage boy to keep his dirty hands to himself, laughing, singing.

Pressed against the Geologist, reaching around him, Ivy touched the latch. And the gate fell open! They fell into the garden. Almost broke their necks on the steps. As they crossed for her door, wrapped up in each other, the security light went on, making their strange endeavour unavoidably obvious.

5.

Shh-shh-shh…

Reeling him in. Reeling Berry back in, back to shore. That familiar sound. A fish on her line. Reeling him into the kitchen. Into the morning. Back to the land of the living, after that terrible night. And out she's rattling his bag of dry breakfast – shh-shh-shh – always three times, in that same way, rule of three, drawing him in, winding him in to come looping and lolling in and out her ankles till she empties the food for him into his bowl. He lowers his head.

It's calmer. He's back in the world. Their world. He's himself again. He can feel himself surface. He's clearing, like a river that was all swirled up with sand now settling, now running clear. The cat's head lowered, the cat's attention occupied with eating, he can hear himself think. He can hear Ivy speaking, hear Ivy thinking:

Him… not like me… like him… was… opening your door… a stray… astray… see… like him… like him… nothing like him… like I like… like I'm like… liked…

like... and lick-lick-lick goes Berry at the food and like-like-like he's thinking.

Creatures of habit, he and she. Living a regular life. Time so regular it's almost still. The only sound his own crunching and slurping. And the man from the night is gone. That thing, that inhuman thing, an obstruction, blocking the whole flow, it looks like it really is gone, like it really was just a terrible dream, and he's gone, and she's here, and they're them.

Now he's hers again. He's all she needs and all she has. He can give himself. She can have him. He can have her scratch at him. *Take Berry to her. Make conscious choices.* One hand of hers strokes him, the other holds her own brow. His head could be hers. Her hand could be his. If he wasn't Berry, if he was a man, could he truly give himself like this?

'Just me, cat,' she says, in confirmation of everything.

Yes, he says. *Just you. Just me. No one else. Just you and me.*

'What a pair!'

Yes, what a pair we are.

She sits at the kitchen table and he walks on the floor on all four of his legs between warmer and cooler places. Through the window, sunlight's slanting, filling the sink with dust and gold. Dancing. Swirling. Kittenish. In and out, in and out of the sink, he dances. When he thinks of her again she isn't there.

But what does that matter? They're back in their old routine. Not like yesterday, not like last night. But like the day before yesterday. And the day before, and the day before, and always and eternally. And the man from the night is gone. The whole excessive, unpleasant, undomesticated hallucination of him, it's gone, really gone.

Then, appallingly, unasked for, again he appears.

Outside the window, coming into view. Appearing from behind a part of building that was hiding him. The man. Coming. Passing. On the grass, on the path. Moving across the garden. But he stops. The big man. Stops. Pauses. Looks around. Looking like he's staked a claim to this land. As still as a tree. His toes might take root. As 'at home' as a tree. As territorial as a tree. He looks towards Ivy's window, Ivy's door. A fresh plaster on his forehead.

It's the man from last night: that's undeniable, unavoidable.

And Berry knows him. Knows he knows him. Knows he knew him. He'd already known him. He'd seen him around, before last night. Another neighbourhood predator to know about. Like those neighbourhood foxes. Like those neighbourhood dogs. A presence of muscle and scent that Berry has always noticed, that he's always known…

Where was he until now, this man? Hiding the whole time behind that wall? Biding his time? When did he leave? When did he come back? Can't keep track. What's he doing here? Can't focus. Tied to this little brain, these animal feelings, dozy or hungry or predatory or afraid...

'Leave,' says Berry, watching at the window. But he's no guard dog.

'Leave,' but the hiss won't pass through glass.

'Leave,' but Berry can't move for fear.

He's seen. The man. He's seen he's being watched, the big man – watches back. *But the way he looks at you, you could be nothing. You may as well be a vase of flowers, an object, nothing.* How come he appeared there? Appearing out of nowhere. How? Through the gate? Over the wall? From out of the flowerbeds?

Maybe he wasn't coming this way; maybe he was up to something else, but now he looks at Berry's window, clearly thinking about the flat, about inside the flat, about Ivy inside the flat. *He'd like to break down my door. I can read him. I can sense him.*

He turns away, shaking his head, turns back. He wants in.

And Berry's about to chase him out, about to go after him, about to, about to, flinching and flinching and frozen and flinching... because if the man tries to get in, if he gets in, if he's let in, if, if, if... because it can't happen, whatever happens, it can't happen.

*

The garden Berry enters is quiet. Vibrating with stillness. The flowerbeds, the grass, the walls. Vibrating. The man isn't anywhere. But it must be a lie. It must be a lie, and the outside's not rid of him. And they need to be rid of him. Fear everywhere. If he enters again, who knows? It might all be over.

So, go. Scramble up the brickwork. Walk the wall. A line between two gardens. Alert to everything. Shimmering leaves. Growling traffic. Let that pigeon hobble away, take flight. At the corner, pause, take everything in. What's out of place? That's it. That's what the man is. A thing out of place. At the corner, wait. Watch the lane below. Look right, towards the road. Left, towards the cherry park. Shivering for warmth. How did he escape, if not by the gate?

Consider options. The drop to the lane. The risks and retreats. And the flat's pulling at him. Calls him back. He never goes far from the flat. But he has to be here. Has to be. Has to. The large man is somewhere.

The threat, it's somewhere in the world. He can sense it, taste it like metal, feel it in his throat, the threat. Shivering. It's colder. It's nearby. The threat. It's now. It's near.

He tenses. Down in the lane, seeing it suddenly: the neighbour cat is walking.

He has the advantage, surely. The higher ground. The advantage, as the neighbour cat approaches, down below. The large, long animal. Beige-coloured in the beige-dirt lane, approaching. It's steady, the neighbour cat. It's paced. Composed. It doesn't look his way. It means him mischief.

The air is hushed and cold. He's gauging the surroundings. They both are. The distances. Distance from the lane to the top of the wall. Distance to the back door. Angles. Geometries. Gravity. Their degrees of strength. Their different sizes. Their teeth and claws and limbs. All the other background noise and information.

But he can't compute. He's an inside-cat. He's inside Berry. Can't read Berry's senses. How do these switches and dials work? Clink-plink-slink, it's tinkling, the neighbour cat's collar-bell, like seconds ticking and skipping as it comes.

You're the weaker of the two, and you know it. And it knows it. You know it like a cat knows. It's nearing your place on the wall, below the wall… Unhurried. And time's unhurried, moving with a measured steadiness.

Moving on long, sleek legs. The colour of sand.

A beautiful animal: the threat.

Drawing you in: the threat.

A moment later, Berry's back inside the kitchen, heart racing, present again. He's here. He's now. He's Berry. Where was he? What was it? The squawking is loud. It's stopped, but he still hears it. There was squawking, a moment ago. There was squawking, there was frenzy.

His own squawks, obviously. He heard them in Berry's head. Berry's muscles and juices, it's all rushing. Beating, beating, his heart's too small for its beating. God, God, God, going and going. Slowing. Jolt-jolt-jolt. Jolt. Jolt. Jolt.

Outside, it's like nothing happened, like there never was the man, like there never was the neighbour cat. Outside it looks like a beautiful morning. And Berry's safe. Settle. Safe. Swirling sand. Settling sand. Settling. Settle. Safe. The neighbour cat can't come through the flap. The neighbour cat can't cross the threshold. Nothing can. *You're safe.* Settle. Stand. Sit. Stay. Settle. He can't settle…

… because the man is in the world. It can't be ignored anymore. He's somewhere, the intruder. And Ivy and Berry aren't alone any longer. It's begun. The siege, like he always feared, like he always knew. It's over, their long solitude. The season of siege has begun.

He's leaving little swishes of blood on the kitchen tiles. His tail is bleeding.

6.

Another strange night at the Southern Royal. Another stranger. Today on the ward, it seems, some kind of crime has been attempted. A chancer has tried their luck. These things happen. People walk in off the street. Of course they do. This is the urgent treatment centre. It's the definition of this place: somewhere strangers with strange histories can walk in off the street... These things happen, missteps like this, whatever it was. Every day, a chance for terrible mistakes, though nothing gets past Ivy, experienced as she is. She's whisker-perfect. She always sees it straight away, what the chancers are after. Their gameplaying. The chess moves of their questions. They're wise and cavalier, the strangers on the ward. And Ivy's wise to them.

But what is it that's happened this time? And when? Ivy can't quite pin it down exactly, talking to the Plain Clothes who's caught hold of her, seeking her insights. He's grabbed her as she moves between a series of jobs.

She's distracted. He's speaking and she's trying to hear. She doesn't have time, so can't quite focus on anything, on his questions, on his face.

Anything? Have you noticed anything, Doctor? Anyone? In recent days. Any telltale signs? Any small detail that stands out? Anything odd, however small? You must have plenty of investigative skill, Doctor, I don't doubt, in your line of work. You must know what to look for. Anyone out of the ordinary? Anything that doesn't sit right? Any suspicious types? *Worse-for-wear* types? *Been-in-the-wars* types? All sorts must come through...

He asked more questions than they usually do, she tells a nurse, later.

'Who?'

The detective. The policeman. Chap with a hat.

'Detective?' says the nurse. 'Police? For what? What incident do you mean, Doctor Dover? There's been no incident today. No causes for concern. No one came about anything like that. Not as far as I've been told. Not that they tell us anything, us nurses! But no, there was no one. Are you sure you've remembered correctly?'

For the rest of Ivy's shift, it keeps stirring her up like a cauldron, this mistake, her mistake, the man tonight... What was he? An officer? A patient? A relative? And what did she say? Was she confidential? Why let him question her? Why not question him? A slip-up. She's slipping. She's been caught slipping.

She tries to picture him, the man, and can't. She tries to hear his voice. Can't. Somehow, she can't recall a single feature of the face. But those other heads she's known... their shapes, their weights, their architecture... those heads, they've left their memories forever in her hands: Keele's injured head, the medical school head...

This man, the Plain Clothes, she can't see him. A featureless, expressionless face. It must be a symptom of whatever's wrong with her. This prosopagnosia. This face blindness. When he left, he'd adjusted that incongruous hat. It wasn't impossible, a hat like that. But unlikely. It had seemed to explain the blank face. Oh, so here was all the character, in the hat!

No, she knows what he was. A hallucination. Delusion. Maladaptive daydreaming. She made him up out thin air. She made him up to question her. A voice in her head. She's slipping. She's caught herself slipping... Where's her head?

The medical school head. You could have called her expressionless, too: Hedda, the woman's head, their first body – their first body part at least – the head assigned to her student group. An old, dead woman. Blank. Lifeless. But you couldn't help reading a lot into her, reading a whole life into her face.

She's withdrawn, you thought. *Inward-looking.*

Nameless, so they named her Hedda. Not a bad pun, and without too much of the gallows jokes you heard a lot of, as a student in a white coat. Who came up with that? Maybe Ivy. It had her own demure, thoughtful, sort of humourless humour to it. *You were seen as fairly feathery back then, fairly flimsy, frail.* They'd pegged her as 'one who won't make it,' those garrulous, frightened males.

Hedda.

It couldn't be true, but Ivy began to see her as a woman from a foreign, northern country, this pale and silver Hedda, brought in from the cold, brought down to the lowlands from a long-lived, snowy life in the tall-treed mountains. Ivy was gentle with her. She was gentle, too, with the full cadaver of a man finally delivered to them. Other students saw it as weakness.

'No stomach for handling guts,' they said. 'No guts for handling stomachs.' But not all of them made it. And she's still here. Here she is, still. They'd never realized about her, not really. They didn't understand, it wasn't caution. It was care. That word – *care* – it means a lot, and she knows everything it means.

The full dead man, it was the first male body she ever saw 'in the flesh', 'in the cold light of day'. She'd never seen Iain Keele's body with the lights on, teenagers in the bedroom of her parents' house. She'd felt its press. She'd thought about it, Keele's body, how she wanted him, and how much, and in what ways. But she'd never seen it, except in the dark, under the covers, an apparition.

'Let's be lovers, Ivy,' she remembers him saying.

Not, 'Be my girlfriend.'

'Let's be lovers.'

And she'd laughed out loud.

Lovers?! People don't have lovers, Keele. We're children, for fuck's sake! Or she'd say, Lovers?! We're adults. We're not kids. Can you stop saying *lovers*? Can't we be grown-up about this? Let's just be very good friends, Keele. Let's keep getting on really well and leave it at that. Let's be better and better friends and let's see…

Then she'd drawn him to her. She'd kissed him there, kissed his head, somewhere on his face, some distance from his lips, her book between them, open in her lap.

In those study sessions in her bedroom, they really did study, she and Keele. Though none of their subjects overlapped, they'd sat together with their books around them, cross-legged on her floor. He wasn't about to get good grades, probably. He was studying her, she knew.

She told him about herself, bit by bit, as if she was opening rooms to him.

She told him how, for example, one spring, slamming the door on her sister, she'd broken her own finger. But rather than rush her to the hospital, her father had brought out supplies and instruments and had taught her to splint it at the dining room table.

This little finger on my right, she said, wiggling it now for him. Then Keele had reached out. He'd held her hand.

And all of a sudden her hand was something else to her. It wasn't hers. He was looking at it. He'd transformed it. Out of place. From another world. It no longer felt like a hand at all.

About Ivy being a doctor, there was never any doubt. Her father had rarely spoken about his job, about the toll, about the losses, about the deaths and the bodies. But downstairs, in her living room, without taking a single book from the shelves, Ivy could say everywhere that held an annotated nude. Open fell the well-thumbed pages...

They were alone. Only Nana was with them – the big, old-lady family cat, Ivy's chaperone when the parents weren't home. Nana sat in the sun of the windowsill, watching them together with her half-closed eyes, seeming to say, *I'll allow it. So far...*

Look, Keele! Ivy called out, locating in one of those books the photograph of a naked man. It stood confidently, lightly. Slim. The paunch of a healthy young father. Cocky. Good-shouldered. A wise and instructional lover. Or: Here, Keele, she said. Here was more biology. Here was a set of finely delineated sexual organs. Her fingertip traced them like a maze, as familiar as her own signature.

But we never talk about it, she said. Dad's never even said the word *sex* to me.

Out of nowhere then, throaty laughter echoed in the fireplace nook. It was her neighbour, beyond the wall. A woman who lives alone, Ivy explained. A woman like that, you know? (And now Ivy wonders, too, about One-Two, another woman who lives alone. A strange woman taking in strange men. She wonders about all those alone women she has known…) A woman like that, you know? she told Keele. I always wonder about her. What does she do all day? Does she like men? Does she like sex? She only laughs that way when her ex-husband visits…

Then they'd stared at the empty hearth, Keele and Ivy, the virginal boy and girl, unable to shake the sense of something there and not there, another presence… Nana, too, had gazed on…

Actually, wouldn't Clover have been in the house, as well? Right at the moment anything might happen between them, Clover would always burst into the room, like too much sunshine, like curtains flung wide, hurling her body between them and calling, 'Hi, Iain! Hi, Sis! What are we up to? What shall we do, us three? I feel so left out!' Then Iain, laughingly, would answer, 'Great timing, Lucky!' and Ivy would shoo her away, saying wasn't Clover a little young to be playing their babysitter?

In the night – one of those nights the parents were away – Ivy went looking for Iain. She entered the guest room. Clover must have been asleep by that point, lost in innocent imaginings beneath her pure, bright sheets. But Ivy got into the guest room, got into Iain's bed, found his limbs, his torso, found him lying, breathing, warm, alive. She couldn't name a single thing that either of them touched.

Hey, Dream-Boy, she said in the darkness. What have you got there?

She realizes, now, that she's home, that she's outside the tenement flat, that it's morning. *Oh, here I am,* she thinks, seeming to re-enter herself coming home with the morning, coming home from her nightshift. How did she get here? When did she get here? When did she leave the hospital? Where was she and what was she doing, all that time at work? *Maladaptive daydreaming.* She's spent the whole shift in a dream.

But she finds herself now coming home, coming along the lane, coming through the gate, crossing the garden, finds herself reaching her door, and finds, laid there at her door, sheltered under the lip of the doorstep, Berry's little gift for her – the mouse, the dead mouse.

No, not a dead mouse. A dying mouse. She sees it before she sees it. She sees a thing. She sees it's a living thing. She sees it's a dying thing. *Ew!* Tiny organs like fruity sweets. Black liquids. Sticky liquids, crisping. What's the purpose of this? What does Berry expect her to do? It can't be the desired effect, her feelings about it.

Stupid creature, she says.

There's sunlight and no sun. A wet, wispy chill clings to the sandstone, to the grass, to her chest. She puts down her bag. Without opening the door, she goes to the gardening trunk on the patio, under the window, and crouches.

She reaches deep, pushing tools aside – shifting, clunking, clattering – to remove a short-handled coal shovel. It's cold in her hand.

Then, clutching the shovel, still squatting, she crab-walks to the flowerbed by the door.

She should be good with any death. So, why this revulsion? She'd rather not touch the ripped mouse. Except, it won't scoop. So, she has to use her fingers, brushing it onto the flat of the shovel. It rolls onto its side, its front, then onto its back again. This is why she prefers to keep the cat indoors. Not for the first time, she wonders, *Is Berry a wild thing?* He didn't arrive in her life in an ordinary way…

What's most sickening isn't the mouse itself but the thought of Berry doing this *for her*. For her, Berry's savagery, Berry's kill. No, not a kill. Not dead yet. A mortal wounding. *Ugh!* Unwanted: dead or alive. And is the cat so dumb it can't tell the difference? No, that's the point. It's the dying that matters. That's what Berry wants to gift her with. It's that it isn't dead yet. That's the red ribbon on it.

She lifts the shovel carefully, like a cup of tea. The mouse is still moving. The paws are open, the small mouth wide. The bared heart flaps like a little pink purse pinned to its breast. So tender and slight. An image of the waking city. It's gone. It has died.

'Hello, Ivy,' says the Geologist, who's been standing there for how long?

'Ivy, hi,' he repeats.

He's standing close by, taking up a lot of the garden. She catches her breath, seeing him again. Or it's just the chill of the morning. She notices again how big he is, remembers the weight of him in her bedroom. His head in her hands. His body upon her. No coat today, a cold day like today. His body is beneath his clothes. He stands still. His breath shows in the air. Steam seems to rise from him.

But isn't it finished with? The two of them. Isn't all that over and done with? It's not normal, is it, to meet again, after an evening like theirs? Admittedly, she isn't sure how it works. Maybe she's the naïve one. And why's he using her name like that, like they know one another? She hasn't said his name yet. It's another thing he has over her. Too late now to say, *Sorry, I don't quite remember*…

'Hi…' she says.

'Grant.'

I know.

They're standing at her closed door. She's holding the mouse out in front of her, level on the coal shovel. Now it's her, not the cat, seeming to offer this gift. But he doesn't say anything about it and doesn't seem to mind if she doesn't know his name.

'You just getting in? Nightshift?'

She nods. What brings you down here?

'Came to see you. How's your spare room?'

Always the suggestion of her rooms, of her beds. She

46

remembers him at the hospital: *You could do that in your sleep.*

Endearing, in a way, how eager he is, what a boy he is.

'Thought I'd take a look,' he says. 'The flood.'

Flood? Oh, yes, my flood.

She must have already told him about it, her flooded spare room. *Sorry about the smell,* she would have said, ashamed about the reek of dampness and, under that – what? – cat smells that cat-owners can't recognize.

'I was passing,' he says. 'Thought I'd stop by. Have a look. Do my part. For the community. Pull my weight.'

Why don't you come in? she says, searching for a reason to keep him out, finding none. Somehow the dead mouse makes it harder. It throws her off.

Again, she has no idea how it happens, or why. But here it is, the way she lets him into her home a second time.

Wait. I should dispose of this, she says, and she moves towards the bin enclosure. Which would it go into? Food waste or general waste?

'Non-recyclable, that's for sure.'

Oh, let's recycle it the old-fashioned way...

Then she flings it, flicking her wrist, so the flimsy body flips from the tip of the shovel, somersaulting up, and down into the flowerbed.

It's his fault. This man. All the Geologist's fault. He brings it out in her, these silly acts of abandon that go nowhere.

But quickly he takes over the shovel – 'May I?' – and, crouching, he uses the corner of the blade to cut a wedge into the soil. He plops the mouse inside and covers it. 'So it won't attract undesirables.'

And now they've held a little burial for it! What is this?

Really, what is this?!

Come in, she says, exasperated with them both. Just enter, Grant. Enter…

With no more ceremony, she shows him through to the spare room.

You'll want to keep your boots on in here. Any insight is appreciated. Do you need tools? Tea?

'Nothing for me.'

She keeps altering the role she gives him: first patient then lover now labourer. But he's never offended, just goes along with everything, talking now with a handyman's banter, playing any part. And always he's himself. Nothing more, nothing less.

'Let's take a look, see what we're dealing with.'

Again, she remembers their first meeting.

Let's take a look at you.

'This it here?' he says. 'Aye, the damp's rising. Got to keep your head above water, eh? Hah! So, let's see what those higher-ups don't want to think about…'

Maybe, in fact, she didn't talk about the flooded floor that night with him. She's been raising it in Residents'

Association emails for weeks, but he isn't a homeowner so he wouldn't be privy to those domestic tussles. Her messages get little response.

'Not their flood, they reckon,' he says. 'The higher-ups, the up-themselves. You'd think they'd notice, all the looking down on us they do. What do they think we are, the live-in help? What's your flat? Just stilts to prop them up?'

It's a bit rich to complain. Ivy's hardly on the poverty line, in this nice building, in this nice neighbourhood. But she likes to hear him say it.

They're both looking at the carpet in the corner of the room, standing side by side. She notices how he fills the space. He could be sizing up the problem. He could have no idea at all. He presses his toe against the darkened weave, rubs his boot where it frays and crumbles, kicks at the wall.

'You know your neighbour on this floor? Wee bald guy. Got the rooms above, too, hasn't he? A duplex, aye? Cox-Coburn, right? Two-storeyed Cox-Coburn. Bet he'd own the whole tenement if he could. Bet he never comes down to this level. His garden entrance is just for trades-men. His lower floor is just for storage and wine and the dog. Just his buffer against rising sea-levels. They're rooms someone could be living in...'

He gets down now to lift the flap of carpet. They look at the hole, the floorboards.

And weariness comes over Ivy in a swell.

'A lot of water,' says the Geologist. 'What time is it? What's the moon up to?'

Sorry?

'Low tide or high tide? Hah.'

Sorry, ha-ha, yes. I'm just tired. I was working. A night-shift, you know. A long night.

This weariness. It's like she hasn't slept in years.

It's like sleep's a new concept she's suddenly learned.

I should go to bed. Can I – would it – if I – a lie down?

She wants to ask if it's strange, leaving him here working while she goes and sleeps. *Strange? Don't start pulling at that thread, Ivy.* The strangeness of all this, of the two of them…

'No bother,' he says. 'Leave me to it.'

As she walks out of the room, she hears him tsking – tut-tut-tut. Going through to her bedroom, she sucks through her teeth – snt, snt, snt – but Berry doesn't appear. *Why does that weirdo cat keep disappearing?*

She gets onto the bed in her clothes, closes her eyes. Surely, she's being too trusting. This man in the house… *Have you got a death wish, Ivy?* She's ready to be smothered as she sleeps. Then, in her dream, she's lying in a boat on the sea at night, down in the hold, the rocking of the boat, the creaking of wood, wood cracking, the Geologist prising up floorboards…

7.

Here for a reason. A reason he's here. *Try to remember,* he thinks, curled around himself, spiralling, under the armchair, licking at the tail where the tip is missing. A reason. A reason. And each electric lick, it sends a zinging up his tongue, down his spine, bursting through all of the hairs of his fur. *Sharpen it,* he tells his cat-brain. *Remember. See it,* lapping the tail like a kitten at milk. And each – lick – each lick, it – lick – it jangles, it – lick – it rings!

A reason he's here. Here for a reason. But it keeps escaping him. One moment, he's awake, desperately awake, inside Berry, knowing he has to watch over Ivy, defend her, keep her... The next, he's a cat, alert to any sudden sound in the street, or caught by the play of shadows on the carpet, or lying in a sunlit window, growing more and more lethargic...

What is it? Do the cat sensations overcome his consciousness? Does the cat-body make up too much of him, and the soul in him can't hold out? Or is it that the cat parts aren't sufficient? Cat-brain, cat-heart, it's not enough to drive his love. If he was human… If he could be her human…

He knows he's a cat. Would a cat know that? He knows he's a small male adult cat, black. He's noticed his method when he urinates; or the yearning washing over him on certain days, in certain seasons, the perfumed blossomings of female felines in the distance. He notices all his animal needs. To hunt. To hide. To reproduce. He notices the neighbour cat. Its dominance. Its sovereignty. He worries about his feelings. His body worries. He can't think through those feelings. He won't. He'll think of Ivy. He'll think of her.

And the threat. There's a threat. But then it's gone. Then here. Then gone again. And he can't quite remember… What was it? When was it? And will it be back? And how will it try to get in this time? Is every entrance barricaded? How to hold out? How to withstand it?

Was it there at all? Is it anything? Is everything his own imagination – the rooms, the woman, the threats, the world? Has he dreamed himself, too? Did Ivy dream him? Is he fading? There seems to be less and less self. He can't grasp the days as they're slipping away. Whole hours passing without awareness. Lost in sleep then in a dream then in a memory then where?

But there are moments, like now, finding the man here a second time, inside again somehow, and Ivy sleeping,

Ivy unguarded, moments like now, coming into a room to find him, and coming to his senses, moments like now when it all becomes certain, when it all comes together, his soulful devotion, his animal instinct, love and hate, manifesting...

Fuck you, you fuck! The big man, there. Fuck him. The big man, in the corner. The fucking big man in the fucking corner. And Berry in the doorway. Berry here. Alive. Evil. Berry saying fucking Christ fucking creep! Berry filling the doorway. Berry growing. Doubling. Swelling. Spitting... You fuck! Get the fuck out! Out! Not a second time. Not again. Not another moment. The fuck out. Now. Now or never. No other moment but now. The moment to fight. The moment to maim.

And the big man has seen him. The big man is standing. The mountain man has turned, turning slowly, turning like a mountain revolving, grinding. Standing above a shipwreck. A rot-black hole. He's climbed out of it. He's found another way in. In through a window. In through the walls. Up from underground. Standing. Rising. Turning away from his shipwrecky hole. Turning towards Berry, noticing Berry, taking it in, this brittle little cat, taking it in his stride. Bemused by it. Amused by it, *by you, Berry.* Then he's approaching. He's coming. *As you speak venom. Shot-full of venom. Righteous with poison...*

You fuck! You fat fuck! You animal! Fucking leave! And he will. Berry can make him. Berry can rid them of him. With enough hate. Enough love. Enough devoted love. Enough evil hate. Berry can. He'll kill himself to kill the man. He'll put his body through it. Now or never. Now, now. *Make myself a reptile. Make myself an ape. Kill myself from the inside out. Vomit up a serpent... Fuckhimfuckhimfuckingfuckhim...*

But: 'Weesht,' says the big man, approaching. 'Weesht... weesht... weesht...' with the sound of a sweeping floor like swish-swash-swish, coming nearer and nearer, gentle, relentless, like a sailboat full-blown, like a big ship, big sails rippling, approaching through the havoc he's been wreaking in the room, huge and calm and just try it, says Berry. Just try it. Try it. Just try it. Make your move.

'What's got into you, buddy?'

Berry bares teeth. Berry is terror. He's madness. He's derangement. Anything but human. Fangs. A maniac's grin. Knives. Tongue. He's the madwoman in the attic. He's the nightmare neighbour cat. Golden. Vicious. He's a jungle monster, striped and ten feet high. And the man keeps coming, keeps growing. The size of him! The weight of him! The smell of him!

No, the man's a mouse. The man's vermin. Make him a mouse. Oust him. He's prey. Prey from the garden. Prey from the flowerbeds. From the wall cavities. From under the floorboards. Send him back there. Send him packing. Because you're the hunter, Berry. Savage hero. Ancient killer. He's coming but you can take him, you can break him. Bring him down. Tear his chest open. Gift the heart to her...

He's here, arriving, crouching, opening out his arm...

Berry bites. Darts claws into the thickness of the forearm.

Bites soft wrist-skin. In his paw – tug of thick arm tearing.

In his mouth, blood, singing.

But he's caught. Whatever he does. Caught. Whatever he does, the giant, with a winking twinge, keeps coming, has a hold of him, and rises again now, gets up again with Berry clamped in his fists. Held. Berry's held. Clawing. Scoring and scoring at the oversized arms. But held. He struggles.

Struggles then deflates. Four legs hang stiff like pipes. A windbag, the big man's instrument. It's over.

Slowly, he sobers up. *Oh, my head.* He comes out of it. Just sober enough to know the state he's in. He sees it now. He had to act, attack, to lose his mind, to lose. No choice, but no hope either. All hope gone now, held by him, suspended, dazed, with this useless body. Can't do a thing with it. Can't even feel it, his body, hanging there.

I'm a joke.

Why didn't the skeleton go to the party?

The story of my life.

'All good, cat?'

He's dandled, can't fight it, the animal in him submissive to a fault. Even with the legs free, he's powerless, a puppet in the grip of those fists, upper body bunched up, foreleg-shoulders hunched, head like a squashed muffin.

It's the end. He has lost.

He's held out, face to face, eye to eye, the fact of the man unavoidable now. Can't look away. Stuck like this. Held. Stopped still. On the big man's bushy forearm, tiny beads of blood start zipping into being – pip-pip-pip – like sewn red threads – pip-pip-pip – quivering on the skin, clinging to the curls of hair.

He's carried out of the room. He's tossed into the hallway, into the air. Landing on his paws, he runs ahead, pauses, looks back, jogs ahead, waits, looks back, keeps his distance, keeps close, as the big man keeps coming, striding through into the kitchen.

'Your mum's sleeping.'

Mum?! My what?! My mum*?!*

It hacks in Berry's throat. Playing that game, is he? No, he's not Ivy's baby, not Ivy's child, not her pet. He's her everything. He's her beating heart. And what about this man? Who does he think he is?

'Let's not wake her,' says the big man. Then from an overhead cupboard a glass is brought out. From the fridge, the milk. The man pours the glass full and then – 'Let me quench. Let me whet' – takes a sip, takes a seat.

And there's the milk in the glass on the table. And Berry won't. He won't drink. He won't be so weak. But he's jumped from the floor to a chair, to the tabletop, despite himself, despising himself, as a cloud starts coming over him, over him, over before he began... He's too wimpy, as he drinks, with lowered head, as his tongue goes reaching and hooking and winding back the slick liquid up into his mouth, through his throat, down to his stomach... and his eyes go rolling around the room. Thoughts swim...

'Oh, are you?' the man says, noticing his drinking, and, 'Should you? Can you? Cats don't drink milk, do they? Never had a pet cat. On the farm, we left them to their own devices. Dogs, we had in the house. My brother. Me. The old man. Dog men. Dogs' best friends. Getting on better with dogs than with each other... You should've seen us, my brother and me, shirts off, and the three big, smelly dogs, all rolling about on that stone floor in that cold kitchen, rolling about on the dog beds and blankets, boxing snouts, biting tails...'

And Berry sees the window. He sees outside. He sees the closed door to the garden. Milk like a moon. The cherry park. His own soft, black feet on the table's surface. The window. A photograph of Iain Keele. The beard of the intruder. Milk.

Seeing milk, he holds on to himself, but it's over. Seeing milk, he listens for his thoughts, but he's too feeble, too tired. And the big man's forearm is forested with hair, twinkly with blood. And the milk, oh, the milk, it's pulling through him like silk through hollow bone.

'Up to you,' says the man. 'But don't tell her. Our secret.'

Then, in good time, Berry's stomach starts to gripe, to squeeze, to tremble, cramping with the awfulness of cow's milk, as he's trying to think, as he's thinking, *Somehow. Somehow. You have to stop him. This man. This wrong man. Any way you can. There must be a way. Find it. Somehow, you have to destroy him. That or be destroyed yourself…*

'That's it, pal,' says the mountain man, meanwhile, stroking him heavily. 'That's it, pal. That's right. Lap it up, pal. Lap, pal. Lap…'

8.

When she wakes: a flurry of messages. All these messages, he's sent them while she slept away the day. She must have shared her number with him. Slowly, she looks over his words, as she carries her phone through to the spare room, now empty of him.

'Given up, sorry,' he's written. 'Who knows where the water's coming from? Below? Above? Sideways? Reckon best get a man in. A proper man. A professional. Sorry about mess.'

The flap of carpet lies turned over. And the soft black, mulchy wood beneath. And the hole, looking wetter, larger, like something's clawing its way in. Something dog-sized and growing ever bigger.

Outside the window it's the same weak light she fell asleep to. It must be early evening.

Does he really live in the building? He seemed to know a lot about everyone. Maybe it's only Ivy who's never noticed him roaming the stairwell, the garden. Has he already been inside everyone else's home? Is he working his way through the house, room by room?

Another message: 'Thinking I'll come back later. Thinking I'll bring dinner. What do you think? Sound all right?'

Maybe it does sound all right, maybe it doesn't. She's staring at the ruined room. It can't have got worse. There's no reasonable way to call him the cause.

No, she won't see him again. It's decided.

A third message: 'Met your cat. Seemed out of sorts.'

The fourth message: 'Not that I know. Just seemed out of sorts. For a cat.'

The fifth message: 'Sorry about its tail.'

It's only then that Ivy locates Berry and sees the injury. It's as though Berry's been just off-stage, all this time, in the wings, waiting to take part. Now in he trots, making his presence known – miaow – and there's the wound. Immediately, Ivy puts it on the Geologist. *What has he done to you?* So, this is the big reveal? The other shoe dropping? This is what he is? A cat-torturer. Psychotic. A thug.

But she knows about wounds. It saves you from losing your senses, all your training. No, the injury is older than a few hours, obviously. A day old, maybe. It's scabbed over at the tip. A gluey muss of fur and blood. Berry's been in a fight.

Hello, sir, she says, scooping up the poor thing.

Lemme lookit ya, m'dear.

Yes, the wound is at least a day old. At least a day old and Ivy hasn't seen it. How did she miss it? She's losing her grip. She should pull herself together, wind herself in, look after herself. Start by looking after the cat. Start by never seeing the Geologist again.

Someone's knocking.

A sixth message: 'Sorry, I'll stop messaging.'

Putting down the poor thing with its wounded tail, she goes through to see. But she's followed to the kitchen by the cat. And when she leans for the handle, she's leapt on. Close at heel, Berry vaults via the worktop onto her back and holds position there, up on her shoulders, where it's never got itself before. Its legs jitter. The claws pulse in and out of her skin.

But she's already opening the door. And looking like this – all witchy, with this crazy-lady, living-dead stole – who'd want visitors? But she's already holding the handle, already tweaking the latch and pulling back the door. She teeters. Unbalanced. An unbalanced woman. *Be careful, Ivy. You can't lose any more balance.*

She's too tall, too narrow. Even her feet are too narrow. She walks on the edges of her feet, a specialist told her, which seemed to explain everything. She ought to have known it herself and put it right years ago, recentred herself, stood herself squarely on the ground. Set herself straight. *You're a doctor, aren't you? You should know better.*

It's the Geologist behind the door, obviously. Uninvited, of course, but he's waiting there in the garden very naturally and patiently, gazing at the heavens.

'Looks like snow,' he says.

She looks up too, steadying herself on the doorframe with one hand. And with the other she reaches to hold the cat in place like she's keeping a hat from blowing away. Now Berry clambers down her forearm to be cradled by her, lying tummy-up in the sling of her arms looking like a big black banana, and all three of them – Mum, Dad and the baby – seem to be gazing up thoughtfully at the clouds.

He's right: it does look like snow. The sky's mucky and heavy.

Yes, look at that sky, she says.

And somehow the word 'sky', *the word for sky,* it has weight to it, too. And it sits there snug with his word 'snow'. His word 'snow', her word 'sky': a pair of solid, sound observations. She could live like this. Talk about weather. Look at the sky. Own a cat. Have a man... It does look like snow. It rarely really does. A good time of year, with the extra weather to talk about.

'I brought dinner,' he says.

He's in a light, date-night shirt and no coat. In his hand are two bottles of red wine, their necks pinched in his fingers like a couple of small beers. Crammed in his armpit are two off-white paper packages. The smell of fish and chips blooms cloudily around them. Tart. Hearty. Sweet. She can't resist it. She feels comfortable and warm but it's only the smell of the food. It's what that smell does to you. She needs to be wary. Where's this leading?

In the kitchen, while they eat, Ivy watches him feed bits of cod to Berry. With that still, calm way of his, he rests his elbow on the table and lets the greasy chunk of fish just perch there in his hand. Snow White, a bluebird on his finger. Carefully, the cat sneaks forward then retreats, the fish-flesh snatching in its jaws. It never surprises the Geologist but, as with everything else, Ivy can't quite tell what he intends.

Not something Berry eats, says Ivy. We live an ascetic life, us two. Do you know what I mean by that? *Ascetic.* Of course you do, I'm sorry. Anyway, we're a couple of nuns, he and I, decked out in black! We don't spoil ourselves. I don't do any of that giving tiny morsels of things like chocolate or butter or cheese, which are all bloody terrible for a cat's digestion.

'Needs fattening up,' says the Geologist.

He scoops the cat into his arms, so it's on its back again. He lifts it to his face and his beard tickles the black belly. Berry looks happy. Amazing how acquiescent the cat is, the legs tucked in, no sign of a claw. It looks like love. A flutter of something like jealousy goes through Ivy. Then she knows what it is. She was seeing herself on her back, herself in his big, bough-like arms, his beard tickling her own soft belly.

'Grow big and strong, cat,' the Geologist says. 'It's a cold, cruel world out there.'

Ivy thinks again of the weather brewing outside.

It looks like snow.

Yes, look at that sky.

'Sky means its own thing in this city,' Keele said once, not long after he'd come to live with her. 'It might as well be another word, up here. I know they speak another language up here, but what I'm saying is it's another language even when it's the *same* language. It's another word, even if it's the same word. You say *sky* in this city and people know what you mean. It means clouds. *Layers* of sky. Greys. Lilacs. Freighted…'

Actually, says Ivy, coming back to the here and now, dragging herself forcibly back, actually, Berry doesn't go outside. A housecat, almost absolutely. Rarely goes out, and never far. Not cut out for it. Look at that tail, after all. In fact – and here she gets up and goes to the door – let's make it official.

She stoops to click the cat-flap locked.

It's like she's closing all three of them in.

Was that a decision? What did she just decide?

And when did she decide it?

Like that first night: *Listen, shall we get a drink?*

When was the decision made?

That's better, she says. Safe and sound. Don't want Berry in another fight. No more drama out there – a pause – not with all the drama in here with us two wild ones.

It's a joke, but the Geologist doesn't laugh. And, looking at him, maybe he *is* a wild man.

He nods slowly, weighing Berry in his arms. 'Seems a little off,' he says. 'Moody,' but what would he know about it? He doesn't know Berry. 'In love, do you think?'

In love?

Ivy's laughing.

In love? Cats don't fall in love! But maybe. Maybe with you, by the look of it! Anyway, it's not the season. It's February he starts getting romantic ideas in his head. And even then it's all for show. I got all his jags and fixes. Made sure of it, the state I found him in, the way he turned up in my life. No, I made sure to get all his fixes and jags. You wouldn't know it, though. Regardless, he gets all emotional every February, every Valentine's Day. But it can't be because of anything. All in his head, silly boy...

Sometimes, I swear... she continues, I swear he doesn't think he's a cat at all. Pets get like that, some people say. They think they're part of the family. They're so brainless.

Maybe Berry thinks that, the way he behaves. I don't know what he sees in the mirror. He seems to have a lot of confusion…

She can feel herself loosening up. The wine. Is this how it went that first night, too? It seems to be happening again. She seems to want it to. It's another step somewhere. It's going somewhere new. Where's it going? It's taking her now. She's falling into him all over again. Can't help it. Drinks flowing. Conversation flowing. It's a river, carrying her. Who knows where it's heading, or why she ever waded in?

To be honest, I sometimes wonder about his inclinations. He's so flirty with me sometimes, aren't you, darling? And Ivy's going with the current of her talk now, floating with it… Fluid cats must be possible, mustn't they? Cats of fluid identities. Cats of all persuasions. It takes all sorts. All kinds of possible animals. That's evolution. I'm not sure he actually likes girl-cats. I'm not sure it's cats he's interested in… Sometimes I find him so… what's the word I'm looking for? Difficult. So *difficult*. Like a man… Hard to see him as a tomcat. Queens and toms, that's what they're called. Toms. Queens. Tells you what we think about cats. And what we think about people, maybe… And what we think about sex…

Sex? Where's she going with this?

Did you know… she begins again.

66

But she pauses. She's getting carried away. Again and again. The wine. She can't keep it together. The wine. And this big, bearded man. Can't keep herself together. She was about to describe the sex lives of cats. She was about to tell him all about it, in fantastic detail, which she probably shouldn't, and won't, of course, won't…

The sex lives of cats. What she was going to say and won't. About the penis of the male cat. About the spines lining the cat's penis. Like a cactus! A cactus instead of a penis! It gets you caught up in all the cat biology. The tongue covered in tiny hooks. Like Velcro! The extra vocal cords, enabling them to purr, like no other living thing! The perfection of purrs! The shimmery eyes, the light inside them like magic. And the eye-slits which gasp like gills. And the tail taking so many shapes (puffed, kinked, rigid), so characterful that the tail is almost talking to you… Animal biology! As interesting as human biology. The genius of it! The life and death of it! A penis like a pufferfish. You couldn't make it up! Penis spines!

'And notice,' Keele would have said, 'that *spine* is an anagram of *penis*…' He seems to say it now, the ghost of his voice interrupting her thoughts, his clever, heartfelt interjections – the heartfelt always lost a little in the cleverness. *Penis, spine, pines. Poems, mopes. Doc, cod. Male, meal. Reside, desire. Cast, scat, cats, acts…*

All for reproductive purposes, she's thinking, those penis spines, there for raking any trace away of other toms. An undeniable logic to it, but unfriendly lovemaking. It makes what we get up to seem tame. Not *we*. I don't mean us, Grant. Not you and me, Grant. I mean human beings. Human sex, in comparison, it's so…

Do you know the word superfecund? A female cat is superfecund. In one litter she can bear the children of more than one male. A complicated love life, for a woman cat. Hard to be a female cat, surrounded by suitors, hard to be chosen, hard to choose… Not how Ivy talks. But she's talking, blurting it out like she's having kittens.

He'll think she's a deviant. Disturbed.

'Superfecund!' he says. 'A great name for a funk band.'

Then he asks about the breed and she says no, Berry's no breed at all. Just common-or-garden cat. But has the Geologist seen the cat that a neighbour owns? The long, sand-coloured cat. A pure-bred. A specimen of the species. A golden statue of a cat. As tall as a table, walking around the neighbourhood, holding its neck as straight as a debutante. So beautiful, you can't imagine stroking it. So beautiful you can't imagine scraps with other cats, because who could bring themselves to touch it? Even when it walks it's like it doesn't want the ground to touch its feet…

But, no, says Ivy. Not Berry. Berry's a mix. Totally mixed up. I couldn't tell you what he is. Don't even know how old he is. I didn't buy him. He wasn't a gift. He just *arrived*. Some years ago. I was alone in the flat. I'd left the back door unlocked. Open. I never do that, but I was distracted. Not my best moment. I had a lot going on. It's no excuse...

Well, I was sitting here at the table, looking at a coffee which I hadn't drunk any of, when I suddenly heard his hellos. And there he was. I guess he'd been meowing for a while. So, I looked at him, and he looked at me. And that was it. That was us.

I don't know his age, but he must be getting on. He seems like a kitten, but he can't be. He looks black, but there's grey in the fur, see – and, brushing behind the cat's ear, she shows a pale, feathery patch the size of a twenty pence piece. Truth be told, he's always had that, as long as I've known him.

'A mystery,' says the Geologist. 'Enigmatic. Like his owner.'

She never expects his charm. Looking at him now, it's a fantastically noble face, you can't deny. Isn't it time to stop calling him unconventionally handsome and just call him handsome? Small, rust-brown bloodspots pepper the sleeve of his shirt. She moves her gaze from his forearm to his forehead. How did he get that head wound? Why didn't she believe 'a sports injury'?

How's your cut?

'This?' he says, rapping his knuckles on his temple. 'Comes with the job.'

What's that supposed to mean? Should she think he hurt it through geology? Was it fieldwork? She sees him slip on scree, his charts going flying. Or he's cracking rocks when his miniature rock hammer ricochets. Or he's shelving minerals in his department... and one of the exhibits... too high, too heavy... frees itself... falls...

It's growing late. Outside, the dark has murk to it. There's ash or feathers falling in the air. *Snow. Sky.* Why not relax into this? The wine. The talk. The river of it. Settle. Stop. Stay. Settle. Sigh. Sail away... She watches that healing cut on his brow, while the cat sits tall between them on the table, like a huge chess piece – the black bishop – watching the both of them.

What are we doing? I don't know what it is. I can't explain it. You and me. Isn't this unusual? This dinner. Is this a date? Are we dating now? I can't figure it out. It's hilarious. You and me. You. Me. Obviously, we don't go together at all.

Immediately, she wishes she hadn't said it, but apologizing will only make it worse.

'I know you think that,' he says, 'that we aren't right for each other. I know you think that. Glad you said that. Not what I think. But you should be honest. You should be yourself. I like you, Ivy, so I like you being yourself. Say whatever you want. I'll never mind it.'

They've finished a whole bottle of wine. Has she really drunk that much? And is it all that much to drink? *How many units?* says the doctor inside her. *What's a unit?* says the patient, trickily. At least she can resist the second bottle, can end the evening here.

'Shall we open another?'

Let's not. Let's just go to bed.

9.

They get in together without their clothes. They don't make love. But she lies hugged against his body like a life-form that lives on another. Her fingers play in the hair of his chest. Again, she can't understand how they ended up this way, again, all over again. But every time she's about to give up on the venture, she keeps on inviting him in.

Still wishing she hadn't said they weren't suited, she says: In this arrangement, we fit together well enough.

They don't make love. Though clearly he could, he makes no move to do so. Is it normal, how he lies there never making a move but maintaining his resolve, gazing up at the ceiling? Doesn't his mighty erection distract him? Wouldn't he want to do something with it, not leave it standing there?

'I'd be a giant,' he's saying. 'Big. Slow... See the mountains and valleys forming... Parts of this country, you can see the mountains moving. If you're still enough. Like it was yesterday. Like it's happening now. A giant could just walk around in it. Thud. Thud. Thud. Pick about in the glacial till. Reach up to the snowline. Wash your face in the fresh snow…'

A giant? She wants to laugh. It's always the same, him opening his heart and her feeling giddy. But it isn't ridicule. She's enjoying him. It's joy.

Above them, where they're gazing, all those other homes are stacked. All those more discerning lives going on, going up and up. Meanwhile, down here, into the night they whisper and murmur like children. The children of the building. The teenagers of the family. The innocents of the city.

'Or, tiny,' he says. 'I'd be small. A wiry, wee guy. Four hundred years ago, maybe. Build my turf-roofed house in the valley. Live slow. Lie low. Watch the seasons change…' He seems to be talking in his sleep. She seems to be dreaming.

'Could have lived like that,' he's saying. 'Up in the valley. Out in the elements. Should have never left, maybe. I've got family, a brother, same as the next guy. Could've not gone far. Not so hugger-mugger, but not deserting them altogether. Could've moved to the next valley. Bought land. Worked my plot. Always thought I'd own some acres, you know? Could've come passed down from the old man, once, but not now – the father I've got, the brother I've got…

'That land. Same soil going back generations. Generations, going down into the earth. It's where I'm from. The land. What I'm from. Owning the land. Owned by the land. Always in touch with the land. Soil under the fingernails. Never thought I'd be so out of touch with it. Never thought I'd be so far from land. Thought I'd never leave. But couldn't've stayed. Couldn't have never left. Wasn't good there. With them. Not good. Had to get away...'

When her phone vibrates, she leaves him in her bed and takes it into the front room. As she talks to her sister, she can see her – pretty Clover – sitting at a mirror with her phone in the dark. Apple-cheeked Clover. Looking lovely like women look. Looking into a mirror in a dark room. The face floating in the mirror, shining like a polished, appley moon... As she talks, Ivy still thinks of him in her bedroom, awake or dreaming, and wonders if he's really in her bed, or if he disappears when she's not there.

She must sound like she wants to get back to him, she must sound like she wants to go, because Clover says, 'Not holding you up, am I? Were you heading out? You should, of course. You're young, Sis. You're free. Not like me.'

In fact, Clover is the younger sister but 'not like me', she says. 'No, I'm a married woman. Not as if *Him Indoors* is about to whisk me away. We've done our whisking – what we ever did of it. No, we did. We did

74

our share of whisking. We whisked! Don't you think we did? But you're a free woman, Ivy. You're living the life. Tell me. Share a little. Let me live vicariously! Let me live the wild life through you!'

Wild? No, but picturing the Geologist through there, in that bed, Ivy thinks, *Is that me? Is that like me? Did I do that?* Now's her chance to tell Clover about him. But what will happen? He might be a total apparition. What will happen if she shares it? It might finally become real. He might vanish completely.

No, nothing to report. Only work and home and sleep, work and home and sleep. But, oh, there was Berry... Berry's tail, but no... Ivy trails off, thinking better of it.

'What about Berry?'

Oh, nothing really, no. Hurt his tail, that's all. Quite badly, but it's nothing. Only a cat, for God's sake! Nothing to write home about. What about you, Clo? How's everyone? How's that brother-in-law of mine? How's my little nephew?

She can nudge Clover that way. She can get her talking. About the husband 'Him Indoors'. About the son 'Tiger'. She can let Clover lead them away on those stories – *Tiger did such and such... Him Indoors said something or other...* using broad colours, beyond believable, a cast of characters in a self-penned soap opera... Then it'll be easier. They'll both be able to relax into their preferred roles, listener and storyteller, doctor and mother...

'No, what about you?' says Clover, this time. 'What about you? I want to know about you. Are you meeting people? Are you meeting men? I know you don't meet men but you should, Ivy. Talking about Iain is good, but we can't always talk about Iain…'

Iain? When did Ivy ever bring up Iain Keele? But Clover's talking now about him again and Ivy's letting her, anything to be silent herself. 'He was funny, wasn't he?' Clover's saying. 'Funny how he still pops into your head, isn't it? I still hear his voice sometimes. Whenever I get home from work. "Welcome home, Lucky!" I hear him calling.'

It's a memory from that first summer, says Clover, the year Ivy and Iain first got together. They had exam leave. Those were the exams Iain the Poet had emphatically failed and had needed to retake, to stay hanging around the hometown Ivy had already left… But during that exam leave they were always in the garden together, Ivy and Iain. Their parents at work. Clover, the younger of the sisters, was still trudging into school every day. Often, when Clover got back, she would find him there, Iain, in her garden, calling, 'Welcome!'

Uh-huh, mm-hm, Ivy says as her sister carries on. It's as if Clover already knows about the Geologist, as if she wants to say, *Wasn't Iain so much better than this stranger you've let in, everything he isn't. It isn't too late, you know, sister. This stranger, you can still be rid of him…*

'He'd ensconced himself at ours,' says Clover. 'Iain. I told him as much. "Ensconced," I said and he said, "What a word! Ensconced!" Part of the furniture, he was. Always there when I got back, saying things like, "Make yourself at home, Clover," or, "Help yourself to anything." Wasn't he funny! He got under your skin...'

Yes, says Ivy, yes, mm-hm.

'He *was* funny, though, wasn't he, Ivy? His thoughts took up a lot of space. I'd come home and he'd be lying in our garden, staring at the sky. Lying in *my* garden. Looking at *my* sky. I'd be huffy with him, like a real little sister. "Working hard?" I'd say, and he'd say, "Actually, Lucky, a poet never rests. I'm working even now." I laughed out loud at that. "I bet!" I said. "No kidding?" I said. "Sounds exhausting," I said...'

Uh-huh, says Ivy, yes and Clover can we not, can we stop, Clover, can we just not talk about him, please, can we just, can we just... just for a moment... can we not?

The next morning, with chilly, refreshing breath in her chest, cosy and humid, Ivy moves towards the Geologist. She'd been dreaming she was swimming. Around the curtains the light has an underwater sheen to it. When she touches him, he starts to shift one way but she guides him on his back, directing his shoulders and hips until he's lying in the centre of the bed, like a deep, dark wood in a valley, gazing up at her.

She sits beside him, one long leg bent, one long leg reaching to the floor, and strokes his belly, his pelvis, his thighs, then closer in, then handling him nicely. *You could do that in your sleep.* He smiles at her and doesn't move. He closes his eyes, breathes in, opens his eyes, breathes out.

Leaning down onto the mattress, raising her knee, twisting her middle, she kisses him. And the bristly mouth surprises her again. She reaches down to fit him into herself, to fit herself onto him. He holds back, going very slowly. She sits a little high. She watches him and sees that, yes, if she puts a tilt into it, he trembles, flutters, gulps.

She leans back. She wants to be looked at. She never did before. She's safe. She's here. She's liking seeing him looking at her. She likes his looking. He looks amazed. She leans back and lifts a little, lifts a little. She closes her eyes and feels his eyes on her. She closes her eyes and lifts her chest. She closes her eyes and bares her throat and swallows with a lengthy, iridescent movement of pleasure.

She wants to stay here, holding on. But at his last moment she falls forward onto him, or she's pulled forward onto him, her face in his broad chest, rocking against him, clinging to him. He calms again. He grows calm again. Another small pulse and he's calm.

She pushes down his knees. She thinks she can. Like so, she presses against him. Like so, she lies very straight, very still. She thinks she can. She's moving. She's still. She can. She's somewhere in the endless landscape of him.

She's dragging fingers through his muscle, his skin. His giant hands hold her shoulders. She pushes against him. She's moving. She's still. She's moving. She's still.

She kisses him to let him know and, afterwards, they get out of the bed and stumble foggily, discovering that, yes, it has, as he predicted, snowed in the night. Conclusively, thickly, whitely, it's snowed. They go cold-footed into the kitchen. They're naked and holding hands. They open the door and see it: the white, walled-in garden.

'Quick' – a rush going through her – 'close it again!'

He shuts the door, puts his arm around her. They turn back inside, move towards the bedroom. From now on, though they can leave, and do leave, they see themselves as wintering together. They see themselves as bandits, hiding out. It's make-believe. As if anyone cares. No one's after them. No one's watching them. No one's thinking anything about the two of them or what this is. But from now on, he sleeps in her bed, like a secret, and they say often to each other, 'We're snowed in.'

10.

All over. No hope. The monster's here, inside your cave. It's found a way in. Already all the ways to save her must have been exhausted. No way to beat the brutal beast. Futile. Nothing to achieve with hisses and claws. Maybe a cat can wound. But the big man didn't mind some spilled blood. Maybe he could scar the arm. The big man could break his back.

After the milk, it's terrible. Berry's body's in an anguish that matches his soul. The fish doesn't help. He throws up in the kitchen, makes a mess of his litter try, causing Ivy to say, 'Yuck! What's got into you? Maybe he's right about you, Berry, and something really is rotten in the state of Denmark.'

What can he do? Knock some things over. Smash some cups and ornaments. She's only likely to think worse of him. An omen. Be an omen. Show 'em. What about shattering Keele's face? Smashing all the Keele pictures – that might be a pithy move. But even if she noticed, who's to say what Keele's ruined face would mean to her?

Does he have nine chances to save her? If so, where's he up to? How many has he spent? *Think*. Lying here, sickened, sapped, he can feel the cat weaken; he can think. So, think. Try to put it in order. The recent days. The days and days and days...

One: The hurt tail. There's that. A narrowly escaped death, and a claim for her love. The hurt tail: she didn't notice. Even taking hold of him, she didn't see it, didn't see him. He's nothing to her: an object, a thing, a utensil. Then, when she did see it, she punished Berry for it, locked the cat-flap, locked him in. So, no, that didn't work.

Two: the mouse. There's the mouse he killed for her. He'd hunted it down for her around the bin enclosure. He'd found it, cornered it. That moment. It was like they'd found each other. The mouse and him. Like they'd always known each other. It knew him. Like he'd known the mountain man when the mountain man came. Like the man is to the cat, the cat was to the mouse. He was its fate. He was its destiny. It had made no move. It had trembled like the pulse in a wrist. Flickered. It flitted left, zipped right. His paw was a faster creature.

After that, after that one true swipe, still brimming with life, overflowing with life, gloriously between two worlds, life and death, the mouse, he'd hoisted it up like a kitten in his maw, in his tender jaws, and he'd laid it at her door. He'd laid it at her feet. *I give you my heart.* Its guts, its gaping guts, its gasps, that was his love for her.

His love for her: she despised it.

And there's the fight with the mountain man. Was that near-death? If he'd been hurt, marked, scarred, wouldn't Ivy have turned on the mountain man then, turned him out? Or is there poison in Berry – venom, sickness – in his teeth, in his spit? Is he infectious? A dirty, good-for-nothing stray. His bacteria. His plague… is it creeping even now into the big man's blood, a trespasser, intruding through the big man's insides? Can he hope?

Then there are the scratches left on the man, the visible scratches on the forearm of the mountain man, reminding (is it possible?) of Keele's injuries. Will she see that? Will she know then? Will everything then come together all at once – the scratches on the arm, then the wound on the big man's head, and then her memory of Keele's injuries, too, of Keele's death, of her love for Keele, of the loss of Keele…? If she could come to her senses… If he could bring her to her senses… If they could both just come to their senses…

How many chances is that? Three? A rattly memory… Nothing to hang a hat on. Taking your soul on faith. This morning, a few hours ago, you could have been a different creature completely, for all you can remember of it…

What else has he tried?
What else can he try?
What else?
What else?

11.

He would write her poems. The boy. She remembers all the words, remembers him speaking them. A young man. Not really a child. But a child. He didn't know he was a man yet, didn't talk like one, didn't move like one. Hadn't left his childhood yet. And she was a girl.

Iain Keele. He would look at her. He would tell her how she looked. He'd seen her, he said, entering the dark corridor, leaving the big-windowed classroom. He had seen her and the spring light had surrounded her. *Light,* he said. It had surrounded her speaking head, as she came through the doorway, spring light fizzing up the long line of her nape where the short brown hair was trimmed close, '…where every one of your million hairs, cut and alive, sent out messages on a wavelength I'd suddenly tuned myself into. My favourite radio station. The perfect pop song. The spring light, Ivy. Oh! Like a flurry of snow.'

She'd turned her head, he said. Coming through the doorway. Finishing what she was saying. She was talking to someone, another girl. She was saying something about science and medicine and school, saying you couldn't learn bodies from textbooks, saying about sex and life and death and bodies, saying she was ready to get started…

God, give me something real! Something alive! Give me a real live thing to dissect!

And as she'd finished speaking, he said, she'd turned her head and ended up smiling right at him. It was like a turning away played in reverse. The odd, unintentional movement, arriving with him. It seemed meant. It seemed meant for him.

But it wasn't, she said. Of course it wasn't. Just an accident.

She felt looked at.

'That night,' he said, 'I dreamt of you in theatre, making incisions. With cutlery, then with your fingers, you sliced up a frog then a butterfly then a fruit. Then the frog was a large and beating human heart, my own, handled so neatly, so cleanly, so keenly.'

God. A real, live thing!

He'd handed her a poem titled 'Going Under'. In it, he was her patient or cadaver. He was lying stretched out on her table. She was working to preserve him. But, cutting him open, all she discovered inside were words, words like 'chest' and 'eye', 'bone' and 'nerve', the word 'heart' in the place of his heart.

I love it. Thank you.

But he wanted more. Wasn't he owed more for his gift? What did she think? What about this half-rhyme here? Or this juxtaposition? What about this word? Does it work, this word? What do you really think? Do you realize this verb might mean more than one thing? It might not even be a verb, at all!

She didn't know.

I don't like to pick things apart.

She didn't understand his gift one bit.

Then she was in her student years, without him. She was existing in her university city, and they weren't together, were they? It was some kind of reformulation or declassification, what they were now. They had moved out of childhood. He should have been at his own university, should have been in his own city, meeting new friends, growing a new life. But when she'd gone to open the door of the flat that evening, there he was. He'd quit his degree, he told her. He'd given up on it.

Something had changed. In his poetry class. A student had read out a poem. 'Spoon', it seemed to have been called. 'I sat listening,' Keele told her. 'Or trying to. It went on forever. It wouldn't end. On and on. Repetitions of the word *spoon*. Spoon!' Keele said now, in imitation.

'Spoo-oo-oon!' And Keele himself seemed to enjoy it, relishing its sound like slow, glowing liquid tipped over the tongue…

But something had snapped, apparently. Keele couldn't stay there. He'd stood up. The other poet had been speaking still, but Keele had stood up and walked straight out of the classroom, walked off the campus, bought a ticket to Ivy's city, so bad had the poem been – 'So self-serving, so self-feeding,' said Keele. 'Dollops and dollops of it' – so clearly had it told Keele what poetry was, what it wasn't, what it was for.

'It's for you, Ivy,' he said, in her doorway now.

They weren't together. But she wasn't with anyone else. No time for anyone else, for anything else but the mastery of medicine; absorbed in her anatomy, in her ethics, in her pathologies… They weren't together but now here they were, together, either side of her doorway. That was the first night they really had sex. It felt so friendly. He'd travelled all that distance to her garden door. Miles he'd travelled to arrive in her bed and lie like an equal, lying like an equals sign. She was a girl version of him, he a boy version of her, parallel, working towards it together, so sweetly.

'I'm yours,' he said, talking all through it. 'I'm this. I'm here. I'm now,' narrating everything. 'Your breasts like bread. Your legs like a long journey. Your toes like kisses.'

I'm yours. You don't need it but I'm yours. You're completely yourself but I'm yours. I'm nothing, Ivy, but I'm yours. If I could be something... If I could be something as completely as you are something... the way you're a doctor... do something so completely... I'll make myself a poem. Every poem will be yours...

But now when she thinks of Keele, she can't help thinking of the Geologist's body, too, transposed upon Keele's body, diminishing Keele's body, overpowering it, that heavy, heaving body of the Geologist. And putting herself against them, against Keele's body and against the Geologist's body, well, how can that be right? Her frail body against Keele's frail body, then the same frail body against the hearty Geologist? It doesn't make sense.

Cognitive dissonance. Bearing simultaneously within you opposing thoughts.

Superfecund. Bearing simultaneously within you the children of opposing males.

It's more and more difficult to understand her younger self. Her choices. Her feelings. She's disembodied from it, from her memories. She sees Keele's sparky, fidgety face, the face that everyone (including Clover) called merciless, the eyes that would simmer or suddenly flash. She remembers his electricity, energizing her. That was something. That was true.

But does she really *feel* the memory? She cringes to think of how he would speak, but she cringes to think of herself, as well. Try to see yourself kindly. She had no idea about anything, that girl, but look on her kindly. Be kind.

Be understanding. *Be a kind and understanding parent to the girl of yourself.* But Ivy can't quite. She's embarrassed by her youth, by their youth. They had no idea what love was, those children.

Then: *What do you mean by that, Ivy? What gives you the right? Who says you know a thing about their feelings? Why would your own feelings even come into it? It was love, if they said so, and if it was love, well, now you've got to live with it. You won't get off that easily. You owe it to him. You owe it to the both of them, him and her. You've made your bed. That's the deal. Now lie in it. She had the love, now you've got the grief. No walking away now.*

The night Keele arrived at her door, she'd already lived here a year. He'd only just started at his university. His school exams had been such a grandiose failure, so caught up in her had he been, that instead of leaving home straightaway he'd had no choice but to stay another year in his mother's house, in his childhood room, taking another run at it. Ivy and any friends of his had all moved on so he'd had to hang out with a younger crowd. (Among them, hilariously, was Ivy's sister Clover! Imagine those two, buddying along together!) So, by the time he'd commenced and renounced academia in one fell swoop, Ivy was already in the thick of becoming a doctor, had already met Hedda, had already met the male cadaver, Doug 'The Unburied'.

She was living in the same flat, back then, with her friends the Historian and the Philosopher. That was Ally and Laine's names for themselves, even though no one had a career yet, or knew anything about their discipline. But, on placements, Ivy was a 'medical student'. Would it ever feel right to call herself Doctor Dover?

The flat had used to have more bedrooms: Ivy, Laine and Ally had each had their own room. Then, when Laine and Ally converged, the flat gained a proper living room but Ivy lost the double bed. It had made sense to offer up her larger room to them, even though she owned the place. Her friends were, to be completely accurate, her tenants.

I know how that sounds, she tells the Geologist now, on the evening sofa. A homeowner at nineteen. A landlord. But house prices were cheaper then, before it got out of control. This area wasn't what it is now. I'm not denying the help from my parents and, yes, they gave the loan interest-free, but I've paid it back already. I know how it looks. The doctor's daughter. The doctor-daughter of a father-doctor and a mother-nurse. I know my demographic. I'm well aware. I know how I look. I know what you're thinking...

But the Geologist just shrugs, puffs his lips a bit tipsily. He lets out a sound like he's trying to concentrate. No, it's clear he doesn't see it like that. He doesn't think like that... It doesn't come into how he thinks about her, just like he doesn't wonder if he's her type, or if she's his type, or if she's one type of person and he another. If only he had the smallest bit of prejudice. But he's simply a little green man from another world, enjoying her, enjoying her manners and movements without context or meaning. He's free.

The truth is – Ivy knows – the Geologist doesn't wonder about her. It's she who wonders about him. She looks again at him. He's in the bow of the sofa, she in the stern. It seems to be how they live now, like they've lived this way for years. His place on the sofa. Her place on the sofa. But it's only been a day. Only a day? Can that be right? The streetlights draw across the window like an orange blind. Snowflakes fall like dust from a shelf. Under the armchair: the cat.

She moves closer to him, rolls herself into the dell of the sofa, into the belly of the sofa, her head now on his knee. She'd like to learn to purr. The snow – she watches it – keeps floating down weightlessly, so much already on the ground, a mass she can't understand. She thinks of a huge, asleep creature, breathing.

'Looks like snow,' he'd said.

She'd almost said, *Well, you brought the weather with you.* But what would that mean? Where *is* he from? What's that accent? Does it sing? Are islands in it? Did he come down from a snowy life in tall-treed mountains?

'Looks like snow,' and that now seems like his first and final arrival. *Looks like snow,* and – click – she'd closed across the cat-flap lock. If he leaves now, she's certain, the snow will melt and he won't return.

'Looks like snow,' he'd said, and she'd seen Keele at the same door, that night he came to stay for good, looking out of place in her doorway.

I'm yours. I'm this.

Everyone was in the kitchen: Ivy, Laine, Ally. Then Keele knocked at the door. They were sitting at their kitchen table. They were sharing a bottle of red wine, a large pan of yellow pasta with orange cheese. Then Keele knocked at the door.

Iain? What are you doing here? Don't you have classes?

'I've quit. I've given up on it.'

Quit? Behind him, the garden was dark and brooding. She stood there, with her long toes tick-tacking a private message to no one on the lip of the doorframe. He'd quit? Could you do that? Ahead of her were years and years more training and challenge, but she couldn't imagine changing her mind, couldn't imagine throwing in the towel, swerving off course.

'It's not for me,' he said. 'I'm not for it. I'm meant for something else.'

At the table, Laine and Ally made eyes at each other. They mewed. They were caught up in their own passions. But where was Ivy's heart, at that moment? Did it swoon? Did it swim? What did she feel?

'I'm for you, Ivy Dover. I'm nothing. I'm yours.'

What overcame her then, there wasn't another word for it but love. It was love, the swell of dread she felt.

'I'm yours,' he said, the night he came to her door; and last night the Geologist had stood on the same threshold and told her, 'It looks like snow.'

12.

What else?

The milk? Was that part of Berry's plan? Was it a play for her sympathy? Did he plot his own sickness? Was that another near-death moment he'd delivered to himself, designed to make her fall in love with him all over again, designed to make her hate the man who fed him? Or was it the man's plan, not Berry's. Did the big man know what milk does? That horribly big man, he's an idiot or he's evil. *He meant it, didn't he, to poison me?*

And before that? Were there other attempts, even before the big man came, other missed chances to bind them together? Berry and Ivy, Ivy and Berry. Try to remember. Get the order right. How much time has passed? How much time is left? It's a myth, nine lives. *You won't last nine attempts. Imagine the injuries amassed – a cut paw, a torn ear, a ripped side, a lost eye...*

And what now? What can he give her now? What can

compare to all that fish and chips and wine and muscled strength and human maleness? What can compete with the mountain man? What now, now the man's always here and the door's always closed?

But don't give in. Go to her. Tonight, go to her. Tonight, she's here and sleeping. Go to her where she's sleeping, the monster beside her. Enter her room. Get on her bed. Put on her chest, between the turned-away breasts, your small furry front feet, like some kind of cute and useless resuscitation attempt. Hold your ground. Speak. Tell her: 'Please, Ivy. Please, hear me this time. Not him, Ivy. Anyone but him. You don't know him. You don't know anything about him – where he's from, what his story is… It isn't too late to be done with him, but it's getting harder. Please hear me. I'm here. Here I am. I'm still here. Real love is here. Real love remains. It's not too late.'

It all comes out as cat noises.

Then: 'Not tonight,' she says, half asleep. 'Not in the mood.'

And she bats him away. She tosses him out, into the hall. The door closes.

But he won't let up. He's begun. He begins it, his prolonged assault. The siege. Unending scraping at her bedroom door. Interminable whines. *Iii-vee! Iii-vee!* Hour on hour. Night upon night. Day upon day. Don't relent. Don't give in. Go on and on. Deprive. Detain. Disrupt. Let her be worn down. Let her reserves diminish. Let her hate you. If she won't love you, let her hate you. Let her hate for you proliferate until everything surrounding her deteriorates, crumbles.

But suddenly – the door opening – out they both come, saying, 'Midnight snack?' and giggling and cooking up an omelette, and dropping eggshells on the floor, laughing, like shameless rabbits messing their own cage... Then someone says, 'Well, if we're awake...'

And the two of them go back to bed and the man is coupling onto her, engulfing, grappling, no, no, no... She can't want it. That writhing she's doing. The stiffening and wriggling. Those whimpers. These are messages for Berry. She's telling him, isn't she, without words? Only he can understand. Only she and Berry. She's urgent. She's pleading to be freed. His queen. Born down upon by a tom. His queen. Possessed by this mammoth, abominable tom.

Then, even worse than keeping him out, they let Berry back on the bed.

'A freaky little threesome,' she says.

And: 'Can't believe I said that!'

And: 'Odd little love triangle, aren't we.'

Then: 'Seriously, I need sleep, if I'm to resemble anything like a doctor tomorrow.'

And they scoop Berry up and sally him forth, through the hallway, into the spare room, and suddenly he's shut up in there, the room with the hole, the smell of rot...

That's where he is now, he realizes, hardly knowing how it happened, stuck here, his cat corporeality, standing, pacing, whinging, useless, while he tries to think and plan and plot.

Nothing works. Not torture. Not attack. Not gifts. The mouse didn't work. Not enough of a kill, is that it? Not a big enough kill. The size of the gesture, was that the problem? A gift with more weight might be needed. A grander death. She needs something bigger. She needs a real sacrifice. What's left open to him?

In the dark, in the room, with the rot, he contemplates it: a final offering – what might be his last hand to play.

13.

We're snowed in, they say, but they do go outside. Leaving, for once, by the front door, they hang around across the street, blowing clouds of breath like smokers at a house party. They watch the building. Looking at her windows, peeping up from below the pavement, Ivy thinks of their two-person party happening inside, down there in Minus One-One. Two persons plus a cat.

Such a nice stack of lives! she says. All kinds of clever folks in this building. A lecturer. A gallery owner. A writer – a successful one! A submariner. Even a doctor, no less! I mean myself, of course. *Doctor* makes sense, doesn't it, in amongst all that? They're good people, honestly. They're a higher class of person. I really did land on my feet in this basement flat. A smarter type of neighbour. People know each other's business but in a good way. You're invested in each other. They've made an investment in me…

He laughs a little and she wonders what he means by laughing. Then she wonders what she meant by all she just said. She hates her neighbours. Why say otherwise?

She backtracks. It isn't perfect. Not sterile. For example, I've heard the cherry park's inhabited. Someone without a home might live there. There are signs. Bottles. Blankets. A folding chair. There are sightings. You hear things.

He says it's probably nothing, or not unusual.

They're standing between two cars, leaning back against the hedge of a bowling green. A street of tall homes and bowling greens. All along this side of the street: square bowling greens covered in snow, like pages of paper, each one with its own members club, its own little wrought-iron arch bearing its name. Ivy tries to think of any club she's ever been a member of, looking up at all the windows of her building.

You know about the Residents' Association, don't you? she goes on. On and on, she goes. Have you ever attended a meeting? I haven't seen you there. But I suppose you wouldn't be, not being an owner. Sorry, I don't mean anything by that. A second-class citizen! No, I'm kidding. You're lucky you're not invited along. It's so political. Cox-Coburn is the chair, but I'm sure that he'd prefer a throne! Everyone's somewhere in the pecking order. A big tree of strange birds, that's what we are. Branches of different heights. Everyone knows their perch. Everyone's looking for purchase. Everyone's got a position to entrench or strengthen. Underhand communications for weeks before the meeting. People looking to rig ballots, seal deals, form alliances...

One-Two, for example. In the lead-up she'll catch hold of me on the street. She'll try working me over, try to garner my support about some grievance or petition. 'We have to stick together,' she'll say, 'look out for one another, we like-minded ladies, we female professionals who live alone...' And on the day of the meeting, she'll pull an about-face, playing another angle. But who cares? I'll go along with her, even though I'm nothing like her, nowhere close to her age, not so alone like she's alone, not lonely like she must be. Who cares? I'll go along, even though I know she feels no real concern for me at all, no real connection to me at all...

Ivy doesn't mention how she once took Keele to a residents' meeting, years ago, at One-Two's flat. What had she been thinking? She brought champagne! She treated her own boyfriend like a debutante, introducing him as *my partner*. 'Not necessary,' One-Two had said, accepting the bottle. 'Not necessary, because only one representative per household is proper. This won't double the vote for you, Minus One-One.' Then she'd hastened the champagne away to her fridge, from whence it had never returned.

Do you think they can see us? says Ivy, looking up at the windows of One-Two's flat, then all the over windows, too. The neighbours, I mean. Which window is yours, for the room you're renting? One-Two is your landlady, did you say? Or, have I remembered wrong? What would you do, if she saw us, if we saw her up there watching us? What about Cox-Coburn in his duplex? He's probably watching from somewhere. He must be. He's got enough windows!

Again, laughing: 'What do you mean, Ivy?' he says. 'What should we do? Run indoors? I don't mind. We can if you like. We can run. Whatever you like.'

Before going back inside, she glances all over the building once more, taking in everyone's rooms. She doesn't see a single interested face except, below, at her own window, looking up at them, the cat.

Actually, see that window up *there,* above the main entrance? Above the door into the stairwell. That window. Did you notice it? Do you think we'll see anyone there? I hope not. It's a false window, you see? There's no room behind it. Not for the flat on the left. Not for the flat on the right. Only there to give symmetry. This tenement has some magic up its sleeves. That window, it backs onto the stairwell, see? There's really nothing there. So, imagine if you saw someone at that window...

'Come on,' he says. 'Let's get back to haunting our own little flat.'

That night, she wakes from troubled sleep unable to move and certain something else is in the room. This something else is not the Geologist about whom, at this moment, she has no memory or awareness. It's something else. It has entered the room. She cannot move.

When she wakes again, the thing is sitting on her chest. It's hunched, shadowy, two green glowing eyes. The weight of it pins her down, where it sits on her sternum. It lowers its head to face her closely. Its jaw hinges open and a voice emerges. A lip-less creature, its mouth doesn't move. The voice – somehow she knows it. The voice, it rises, vibrating, rolling, from the folds and creases and gurgle of the throat, words forming out of ripples and growls, a pulsing and trembling going through her in the darkness as she starts to lift now from the bed, to levitate, her limbs like kites, her organs like vapour...

Ffeeel me. Ffeeel me. Bevvare ov him, Ivee. He comes vrrom vviolence, Ivee. A strrangerr. Coming vrrom mountains. Coming vrrom cavves. Vrrom the cold. Dark depffs of cold. Bevvare iff the cold sets in, Ivee. Alllmost too late. But he vvon't leaf you, iff the cold sets in. Ffearr him, Ivee. Trremble. Vvibrrate. Casst him out. Casst him out...

In the morning, she sensibly diagnoses it as 'isolated sleep paralysis', not something she normally suffers from and brought on, no doubt, by too much overtime and a mishmash of dayshifts and nightshifts, and other recent irregularities in her life. The sensation of an intruder, the inability to move, the monster on your chest, the sexual element: it's textbook.

Ivy, where's this going? Where are you going with this? If you knew the ending of the story... What's got into you? You're the old woman who swallowed a fly.

There once was a woman who took in a cat.

Imagine that. She took in a cat.

There once was a woman who took in a man...

A type of poem called a cumulative, Keele once told her. It escalates. It spirals. It grows and grows, spiralling outwards, spiralling inwards...

The Geologist has settled in her flat like snow. Coming back to him is like coming back home. If she's at the hospital, he'll be there, in her flat. If she isn't at the hospital, they'll be together in her home. At some point, he'll pour drinks. Conversation flows easily, inconsequentially. But no one learns anything about anyone.

Then: he's been in the kitchen. He cooks big pieces of meat with no small amount of skill. *Mm-mm, it's like jelly! Oh, it's sliding off the bone!* These are her exclamations of pleasure. Later: he dances. *Imagine that!* He'll drag up something stupid on his phone, pull her to him and sail her around. He's a heavy wave in the sea, swinging you up, swallowing you down...

Does he fall a lot? More than once, in the throes of dancing, he throws out his footing and goes colliding with a piece of furniture – crash – like a toddler. 'An inner ear thing,' he'll say. 'Poor motor skills. An inherited condition. My brother has it.'

Yeah, right. The best medicine is to sleep it off!

If he's drunk often, he doesn't mind being drunk, and she doesn't mind either. Is it a warning sign? Is it another sign she should end it? And does he have no home or job to go to; is that another sign to finish it?

But how to end it, if it's not a relationship? How to end it, if it has never started? And if it isn't going to last, why end it right now? Not important. No big thing. It's just that she likes having him here, here when she leaves, here when she returns. She'll be surprised when he isn't.

We're snowed in, she'd said, that first morning.

It looks like snow.

Look at that sky.

We're snowed in.

'Back to bed then,' he'd answered. A seductive tone. Sleepy and growly. A hibernating bear. And she's decided to hibernate with him. He's a cave she's hibernating in. She's decided to hide from the world with him, and why not? She was already hiding, but now here's somebody to hide together with. He's the wintry mountain she's holed up on.

Some nights (those nights when she's working days), they lie awake in bed together. They don't need sleep, the dreamy way they're living. Some days (if she's on nights), it's like it's night all day in the bedroom. They don't get up. The singing of the shut-in cat sounds faraway. That snowy glow at the window, it makes a gloaming that begins at noon. It's another world.

They can make it themselves. They can make it their own. Has it been two weeks? More? No, only one, isn't it? A handful of days. It feels like forever. It can't last. That way she floated into this, she's floating in it now forever. But they aren't really snowed in, of course. They can leave whenever they want. None of it's necessary. The snow's complicit.

There's three of us involved, she thinks.

Him.

And me.

And the snow.

She feels like a child. She lets him try out pet names. Blossom. Bud. Bug. She lets him lift her. Dancing again, he lifts her right off the ground. How's that, as a way to be? Is the balance off? 'I think it's healthy,' she hears Clover saying. But would Clover really say that about this? No, not healthy. Not helpful. How was it with Keele? How should it be?

Then Clover calls.

'Him Indoors has done it! A breakthrough. My chap! His efforts are finally really coming together. I know, I know, Sis: a long time coming, you'll say. But just think, Ivy! Just think, if it all panned out... if it was a roaring and raging success… Well, this morning, Hubby comes bursting out of his workroom so pleased, and do you know what it was…? No, I don't either! Who knows what it was? But it must have been good, it must have gone well, because he swept Tiger straight out the house. Off to the park with them! Off with their bods! Happy-go-lucky Hubby! There with all the other kids! All the other dads! A perfect sky, where we are. Cold and perfect. Turning out nice! More and more nice! I went to meet them. I was almost there. But I stopped. I couldn't. I'd clocked them. And I just couldn't. They looked so perfect. So happy and silly. What a couple of boys they are! Best buds. And I couldn't. I couldn't risk it.

'Just now, why I called… I was thinking of them, Ivy. All our lads. Tiger and Him Indoors and Dad and Iain. All those chaps of ours. All so serious, aren't they? Always being such *men* about whatever it is they're doing. *Good afternoon, yes, what a serious gentleman I am…* But somehow we see them. We *get* them, don't we? We know, don't we, Ivy? We see what they're like. See how good they are. See that they're good. Good, *good* men. I always picture them all together as a gang. Ragtag gang of lads, that lot. They're not. I know they're not. They don't really talk… But that's what I picture. All our boys together. You agree, right? Don't you agree? That they're good? That they're good men? You do, don't you, Ivy? Because they are. They were. Will be. We chose well, didn't we?

We've done well, haven't we, Ivy? With these men in our lives? These solid blokes. Well done us! We can be happy about that, I think. We can pat ourselves on the back. I think we ought to be happy about it…'

Ivy doesn't mention the Geologist.

She has never named him.

Then she's curled up against him again. So easy to be like this now. So easy to be. He reads from his industry magazine. A meaningless sea you can float in. Words surface. *Volcanic. Oceanic. Atmospheric. Abyssal… Comets. Crystals. Supercontinents…* He travels her across the world. Landscapes green and bleak. Red, dry mountain ranges. Sheer cliffs of ice. Deep-sea canyons. Far-off reaches. Blackness. Planets. Moons.

The night we met… she says. I'm thinking of the night we met. Like it was another time. The time we met, I didn't know what kind of night it was. A dark night, I thought. I wasn't acting that way, like it was dark, like it was sad. I treated it like an ordinary shift. I treat every patient that way. I treat everyone as they come, or I mean to. I was acting professionally. That's how I am, day to day. Professional, even when I'm not at work. But really I thought it was a dark, bad night.

Can I tell you about a death, okay? A boy had died. On the ward. A bad day. There was no hope. He was gone. Brain dead. Dead. We only had to say the word. No one was to blame. But it's tough to take. Death's not easy for anyone, is it? Not for doctors, either. So, when a boy dies on your ward, on your watch, well, maybe it gets to you. Maybe it gets in. Maybe it has echoes in your own life.

That's what everything's about then, a day like that, when there's a death. It means more work, forms to fill in, time spent following up, but that's not what it is. What it is, when there's a death, it colours everything. All through work, everything's an echo of that, an answer to that. It's what I thought you were. An echo. I thought you were about the boy. I think my going with you was about the boy dying. That wasn't fair to you. It was a bad night. It was bad of me. I'm not a good woman. You should know that. You should understand that.

She doesn't mention Iain Keele.

She has never named him.

14.

Locked cat-flap. Locked in this flat. Locked in this cat. A mousetrap. A housecat. A house-trap. Whenever the door opens – Snap! – it shuts immediately. It opens. Flash! A gasp of air. A flood of light. The glaring, snowy garden. Pupils slit-swell-slit. Bright, night, bright, night. Gone. Done. Dark. The door is shut again.

Home again, it's the intruder. The mountain man. Always him. Always here. Here more and more. Gone less and less. Gone less long than Ivy. *Ivy, where are you?* So many hours of just these two. The man and Berry. Berry and the man. Stuck here together.

What a pair!

Always, you sense the arrival. Sense him before he's here. Know it before you know it. His humph. His heft. His trudge. In the lane. At the gate. On the path. At the door. The moment it opens, you're already running for the outside but – 'Oh no you don't, cat!' – you're scooped up, hooked up, crooked up by a booted foot, and swept up and swung up and slung upwards and backwards into the kitchen, into the flat.

He takes up space. He swallows space. In the front room, he sits on the carpet, leaning back against Berry's chair. The big man. Staking his claim. Flapping up his laptop, then he's typing. His hands rattling. A sound like pebbles. Tock-tick-tock-tock-tick. Time's in disarray. Always the two of them. Tick-tick-tock-tock-tick-tick-tick. Stuck together. Stuck to him. Trying to leave, to slink away. Places he could hide. Undersides, corners, edges, gaps. He could disappear into the building, live like a stray or however he used to, disappear forever.

But he stays here watching the big man writing. He thinks he can read, but he can't. He can't decipher the screen. It's just light. A white flame. It's a scuttle of words, but no meaning. Rows and rows of words and words…

For a moment, there's something beautiful. Glimpsed on the laptop. As the man pauses… As the man moves the laptop from his lap to the floor… A patchwork of pictures. A blue bay. Streets of colourful wooden homes. Green trees. Grey cliffs. Grey plazas and quays. And a whiteness to everything. A stillness…

'Like a holiday, could be,' says the man to himself.

And Berry's transported there. Berry's gambolling on that white and multicoloured street. And Ivy gathers him up, kissing his frosty paws. And she carries him like

firewood through the snow. Footsteps in the whiteness…
Crunch-crumple-crunch along the snowy road they go.
The smell of her, like old books, fresh baking, spring
leaves. The warmth of her…

The warm lap. The big man's laptop's open on the
floor. The big man's lap, left open. Lap left warm. A warm
welcome. *Climb onto it. Climb into it. Can't help your-*
self. Hate yourself, but can't help yourself. So easy, so
natural, climbing into the lap, like eating, like sleeping, a
weakening inside…

Not giving in. Not giving up, but it's hard to hold on,
and the lap is so warm… Nothing he can do. Never was.
Never will be. He's nothing. He's nowhere. He's floating. He's somewhere in the room. He seems to be seeing
himself, the cat, there in the big man's lap. Nothing he
ever could do. Not his part to play.

He sees that now. He's only part of it. He seems to be
two beings. He's the body and the soul. And the soul…
his soul's a promise. And the body – it's an omen. The
promise and the omen… Nothing he can do. Nothing he
was ever meant to do. All the promise can do is forebear.
All the omen can do is forebode.

There must be a third. That's it. What they're waiting
for. The thing that will do it. The nemesis, that must be
it. It's coming. He suddenly knows it. The moment to end
everything. It's lying in wait, like a set trap, like a croco-
dile's jaws, it's coming.

First the promise.

Then the omen.

Finally, the nemesis.

It's coming to save her. It's coming to rid them of him. It's coming to draw him outside. It will conjure a blizzard, conjure chaos. It will pull a great cherry tree down on the man, crushing his body, crushing even that buttressed, unbreakable body. It will split his scar open, split his skull open, nose to crown, and the dumb brains going slopping all over the place.

Yes, that's it, the third being, the nemesis, it's on its way… So just wait for the moment, while the lap warms you, while the laptop shows its line of houses standing on this snowy ground as hard and as pure as a diamond, the lie to the violence of winter… It's wonderful.

Berry's the harbinger of death.

15.

Their last evening.

They go out. They stretch wiry gizmos under their boots then stomp through the garden and into the lane. It must be their last evening, mustn't it? It's about to be Christmas. They're about to say goodbye for Christmas and forever.

Finding their way to the thoroughfares, they slip and slosh together up the same high street she walked down with him that first night. That night, the city had been mild and dry, the buildings like crisp yellow leaves. The stillness had rung in her head like a bell.

But now, though it doesn't snow or rain, an icy dampness creeps up their sleeves and down their collars. The kerbs are banked with a black, chunky sod. The buildings are worn-down, their sandstone carvings all crumbly and mulchy. It's too squelchy, too shivery, too real. It draws her closer to him.

He feels real, too. She knows his scent now. What is it? Wild garlic and wet straw and sweaty leather and who knows what? She lets him lead her, unseeing, hugged up close to him. She might really have closed her eyes. He isn't whatever she imagined for herself, not what she ever imagined for herself. She has no clue who she is or what she desires.

There's cold and damp and bustle outside her body, but she's inside herself, looking around inside herself, feeling around inside. She tries reading her heart, her stomach, her knees, every part of herself – her crotch, her throat, her fingers… Is it really this she wants? To feel forever so simply, so unthinkingly, so immediately? Hard to get out of your head. Hard to see yourself from the outside. Hard to see from the inside, too.

She realizes that she's Hedda, the bodiless woman. Of course she is, and always was. A disembodied female head. As pale as silver. Noble-looking. Distant. Disembodied. Very disembodied. Cold. Foreign-seeming. Observed from the outside. Strange, from the outside. Touched. Handled. Investigated. Never revealing its true character. It could be anybody's head.

'Here we are,' he says.

If her eyes were closed, she opens them and sees that, yes, they're here, back at Fair Isle, the same church-pub they went to that first night. They walk up the broad steps and in, under the stone arch. A chandelier of electric candles. A soundtrack of city bands sounding like medieval revelry. On the walls are murals of lovers. Naked men and women with attractive, androgenous bodies, soft eyes, red lips, strong noses. And forest animals. Stars. Moons. Words. Torn flags. Vines sprouting full, heart-shaped leaves...

At the bar, men move out his way. She wriggles in with him, like a creeper. He says, 'What will you have?' And a woman to his right, overlooking Ivy, says, 'Your treat is it, pet? Let me see. Let me see,' stepping back a little. 'What do I want? What's my thirst for?'

As this woman speaks, she moves her head to mean maybe the shelf of whiskies or maybe the Geologist, trailing her eyes over the varnished wood, the amber liquid, the Geologist's arms. Or, is Ivy imagining that? Is the Geologist wanted by women?

'You're a tall proposition, aren't you?' this woman says with great appetite. 'I know I shouldn't. My eyes are bigger than my stomach, darlin'. But you're bringing out the mountaineer in me, I must admit.'

He laughs. 'Let me buy you that drink.'

What is he? A flirt, or a pushover?

You have presence, Ivy tells him, when they've found a seat together, she with her white wine, he with his whisky, his beer. She's shooting glances at the bar, where the woman's laughing loudly. Everyone's laughing and talking and calling out into the evening... But the

Geologist is turned towards Ivy, towards his beer, making good progress with his beer.

At the bar, there. People notice you. Do you see them all clearing out of your way?

He doesn't think of it like that.

'Not all it's cracked up to be,' he says. 'You're always encroaching on someone. Always blocking someone's view. It gives you a stoop.'

She can imagine it wouldn't feel good, no, knowing you're taking up too much space. Meanwhile, Ivy's been living a little transparently, a little invisibly, a little cloudily. She's found wispy by people. She's found un-arousing by both women and men.

Clover set her up once, not long after Keele. The man had treated her well, chatted her up a good amount, flattered her, generously, and she'd left thinking it went all right. But when Clover saw him later (so she told Ivy) and asked him, 'Well, you met my sister? Isn't she perfect? How was it?' he'd replied, 'Yes, fine. No, I liked her. She's attractive, obviously. Tall. She's very thin. She's obviously attractive. I don't think I'm what she's looking for.'

It's something women often tell her (but what a thing for Ivy to complain about!): 'So thin! Where does it go? Those legs! I wish I had your figure.' But it was only that first night with the Geologist that someone seemed to want her body so absolutely and directly and wordlessly.

She'd felt like a well he wanted to drink and drink from. A big man like that, devouring her!

'Some men don't like it, a guy my size,' he says.

She sees the truth of it later in the evening.

'Another?' he says. Then, returning from the bar, he steps into the path of a drinker.

A little spill.

Ivy sees it happen.

'Watch yourself, big fellah,' says the drunk. Then, taking a beat, he looks the Geologist up and down. It's just like the woman earlier. Sizing him up. His size is an aggravation. Whatever they're after, the drunk and the flirt, it's more or less the same.

The challenge hangs there.

Watch yourself.

Ivy's afraid. Violence seems close. Violence at the edge of things. Violence beneath the frozen surface. What if it broke out? It's close, and she's always been close to it, treating its aftermath, treating the wounds of those late-night men, treating the Geologist's head... It frightens her. She's thrilled.

Then: 'No, you're all right,' says the drunk, laughing.

'Just this once,' says the laughing drunk, a hand on his shoulder.

'Just watch yourself.'

And all of it, it's the punctuation of threat. It's the gilding of it.

The words.

The laugh.

The hand.

When the Geologist reaches their table again, Ivy stands. She takes his head. This is never going to last, but the kiss is a message. *Look,* she's telling the bar-drunk and the bar-flirt. *Look. He's somebody's man.* She kisses the head like a provocation.

That'll do it. They'll notice that. She knows her cachet, her capital. Sort of thought of as sought-after. Her tidy presentation, her tight features, her withheld way of speaking, her thinness… 'You look like a certain type of movie star,' Keele said once, 'in certain lights.'

A woman with class. A dry, temperate description, suitable for a lady doctor and her sterilized equipment, her standardized procedures. Men don't want it in women. Women don't want it in themselves. But it's winding up the drunk. She sees it, looking out the corner of her eye, her mouth stuffed up, as she kisses and kisses. It's getting to the drunk. She doesn't attract him. He doesn't want her. But he wants to hit somebody.

Let him. Let them think what they like. Let them think again. Let's really blow their minds, and let's dance.

'What? Here? To what music?'

To the music. There's music.

'Hardly, with all this noise.'

Let's dance like we do at home, she says. Fling me

around. Toss me around. Throw me about a bit. Then she clings to him. She swings with him. She lifts both feet from the ground. She's sexy. She has a body. The room knows. Blood's pumping through every last corner. He's taking her lead.

See? she's saying to everyone. *See? You thought I was one kind of woman. You thought he was one kind of man. You thought he didn't have looks and he didn't have charm, not as much as he has, not all of the charm that he has! You thought he was thick in every sense. Thick through and through! But look at the sort of woman who loves him.*

Not that she does love him. She doesn't. It isn't love. But how she likes to hold his head. From that very first night, from that very first moment, stitching him. Its size! Its shape! A museum exhibit on a private tour. Then the curator says, 'Would you like to hold it?' and you have it in your hands. And you say, 'I never imagined this is what it would weigh! It's so different, to actually handle it.'

So calming, putting your face to him, like putting your forehead against a horse's nose... Stop, Ivy. Stop. You have to stop this. It isn't a horse. It isn't a dog or a bear or a forest or mountain or ocean. He's a man, and you don't know him or understand him, and you certainly don't love him. Be fair. Christmas is coming. Tomorrow he'll leave for Christmas, then you'll leave for Christmas, and you'll both agree that's it. That's the end. Turn away.

Go back to your sadness. Go back to your sad life. Don't spread the contagion. This is over and done with. This is nearing its end. The end is near. But, oh, how I like to have him near…

16.

The warm lap. The lap warm. Warmth swarming. In the dormant valley of the mountain man. In the warm burrow of the mountain man. Marrow melting like tallow. In the warm warren, slumbering, swelling, mellowing, wallowing, swallowing, allowing… How many days has it been? How many warm laps? Lap upon lap. Lapping himself. *Lap, pal, lap…*

'You're a lot to live up to,' the big man says.

Who's he talking to?

'A lot to live up to… Not that she's said anything. Not even your name.'

He's reached forward, where he's sitting against Berry's chair, where Berry's sitting warming and purring in his lap. He's holding a picture of Iain Keele.

'You could be anyone,' he's saying, speaking to the photograph. 'But isn't it obvious? All these photos? I know who you are… Everything I'm not, that's who.

What's the secret to it, mate? How did you find your way in?'

Now he's talking to Berry, not Keele, stroking Berry, looking at Berry.

'How'd you do it? How'd you get her? How'd you get her to really like you, really let you in? I'm "in", I know. But I'm not *in*… You know her better than anyone, don't you? Talks to you, doesn't she? You'll share it, won't you? What's the big mystery? Help me out…'

And Berry lies listening in the lap. An omen. Biding his time. Meaning the mountain man ill will, meaning him bad luck… *Crossing your path, I bring bad luck. Walking towards you, I bring bad luck. Walking away, I take good luck away. Every last bit of luck, I take away…*

'It's serious,' the mountain man is saying. 'It's serious, if that makes a difference. Sounds dumb, I know. Never claimed to be a clever guy. Not fooling myself. Blood from a stone, getting feelings out of me. Feelings… The old man didn't go in for them. Put you to task, he did. The old man. That's for sure. Sheep. Boat. Clearing. Fixing walls. Fences. Engines…

'Never thought I'd be living down here. Living like this. A doctor, too, by the way! Doctor of Geology. Professorial. Me! And a landowner. Or might've been, could be, in the will. Always in the family: our land. I'm high-born, you know that? Born in a mountain bothy! What's higher born than that? Hah! But look at me now.

Educated. Enlightened. Metropolitan! Dad wouldn't know me. Knox barely did.

'That's my brother. Knox. Said he didn't know me, when he came, when we last spoke, when he tracked me down, when he cracked my nut. Knox and Grant. Sturdy couple of lugs, we are. Always were. More like a pair of hills than two men. Built that way. How Dad wanted us. Never meant to have softness. Brought up strong. Brought up rough.'

Berry sees it – a landscape of slopes and stones and mud and scrub – sees an old man building with wet clods, a peasant Frankenstein making misshapen, oversized sons of clay, slapping and slopping on more and more mud and shoring them up like hillforts, reinforcing and hardening them with beatings at their flanks, their trunks. Is that how the monster was made?

'Rough,' says the man. 'How I saw myself. Rough. Strong. Thought I was stupid. Took it for granted I was. But now and then I'd shock myself. Ever find that? Think you're one way then... who's this? Is this me? No, course not. You're a cat! But at school... Geography, Chemistry, History... I'd stump them. The sirs and misses. We drew rain cycles and sir said mine was wrong and I said no, this is how rain moves in my valley. These ridges, these slopes, these burns, these clouds, this is right, I said.

'Same day, I went up from the farm. Clouds inside the house, so I didn't go in but went up in the valley. Got a good height. Followed the stream to the waterfall. To where the waterfall comes down the cliff in a big white trickle. Don't know why but I reached in the pool. Took out a rock. Cursed them all. Cursed the whole world and slung it at the cliff. Cracked in two. Crystals inside. Amethyst.'

Berry sees him. Huge in a huge landscape. Huge, but almost dwarfed in his huge habitat, as he goes out into it, as he clambers up into it, as Berry's eye expands. A crow's eye view. Berry soaring above, sweeping over it. Below: a man in a vast landscape. Berry sees him, at the foot of a waterfall that pours from a clifftop shrouded in cloud. It looks like a rope you can climb to the sky. And the man is a giant at the base of his own beanstalk.

Berry sees him, reaching into the pool, scooping out the spherical stone. And when he launches it at the rock-face, Berry imagines an ogrish yowl. It echoes from the valley. The rock cracks in two like a coconut. Inside: all these purply, glassy, toothy jewels, winking at the dumb-founded oaf… But the man wasn't a simpleton, was he? Not simple. He was a boulder. Hidden inside him, precious stones might glint…

'Got good grades,' he continues. 'Took me down out of the valley. Got out. Knox, my brother. Never got himself away. Not really. Even if he leaves. Not really. Always goes back to it. Too much like the old man, Knox is. Always coming to a head. Butting heads. Giving their share. Good as they get. Gets bad. Knox and the old man. Coming for me, too. But it's not in me. Don't know why. I'm the biggest of the lot of us, but it's not in me. It's in them. They're in it. Dragging me into it, whatever I do. Might've been different with a mother.'

Berry goes on letting himself be stroked. Berry gives nothing away. He could be entirely asleep. He could be entirely empty. He's warm. He's still. He's the warm, still heart of something, vibrating at a molecular level, lulling the world into a false sense of security.

'Jeeze-o, look at me,' says the big man. 'I'm a fool! Baring my soul to you. To you and not to her. Not to the woman of my dreams. But to her pet! Never talked to a cat before. Not like this. Not like the animal could understand. Never talked like this on the farm. Dad's dogs, livestock, his sons: you're a worker, first thing. Cats are mousers. Rat-catchers. Never taught that animals were people. Never taught that *people* were people! Never lived like you two. Never met a woman like her or a cat like you. I like talking to you, cat. You'll steer me right, won't you?'

What an imbecile!

A voice laughs, inside Berry.

'You're a package deal,' says the man. 'Kid from a previous marriage. Well, I'm buying into it. All of it. Was she with him, when you got here? The one who came before me, did you know him? We get on, don't we, you and me? You're good to me. You can trust me, cat. Not taking anyone's place. Don't believe in it. Taking…' He's coming up with something. 'It's not about taking…' He's mustering profundity from deep within. 'It's something you give.'

Bloody idiot.

'The night she took me in…' he says. 'Afterwards, don't know why, don't know where now, but I brought down from my room one half of the amethyst geode and buried it in the garden. Bloody idiot, right?'

A fool.

… But be lovely, Berry. Make him love you. Make him think you love him. Make him care for you like he cares for Ivy. Let him think of you as Ivy. Embody her. One and the same. Ivy and you. Make him a lover of cats. Make him think a cat can love. Make him want you safe. Make him think of you as his safety. Make him dull and dumb and warm, so he'll follow you out into danger, into risk, into dead ends, pitfalls, fatal drops, over treacherous terrain. Make him trust you, and wait for when he'll follow you out to the point of no return…

'Push is coming to shove, cat. I'm going to have to tell her.'

The next day, the man is completely gone.

Then Ivy is completely gone.

For days in the flat, Berry's alone.

17.

Where will you be while I'm away?

'Mind if I set up camp on your sofa?'

Mind if you...?

'No, hah, no. Seeing family, of course.'

Family?

'Aye. Isn't that what people do at Christmas?'

And you're seeing yours?

'I do have a family, you know. Didn't just spring up from the ground.'

And whereabouts do they stay?

'Oh, not far. As the crow flies.'

You have a brother, did you say?

'Did I? I do. Last I checked. So does he, last he checked.'

She tells him the day she'll be leaving and, reading her meaning, he's gone the day before. But if he'd remained, if she'd left and he'd remained, it might have helped. It might have let her realize what this was, that this was peculiar. Then she could have said, No, that's it, this isn't normal, get out. But he leaves before she does. They say goodbye. They say they'll see each other again in the new year. They won't. She's sure it's over.

Before she sets off for the south, for her parents' cottage and Clover and Him Indoors and Tiger the Nephew, and all of that, she speaks to her neighbours. With Cox-Coburn (Mr Duplex) she raises the flood. Her emails haven't been answered. Why not? What is she? Strange noises from the basement? Is she something unsavoury, best ignored? *You need to explain yourself! What are you playing at? Out with it!* No, not how she talks. She'll manoeuvre towards a solution.

She doesn't knock on his garden door – he wouldn't be down there, anyway – but goes out of her own front door, climbs up to the street then ascends the short flight of steps to his private entrance. Through his windows, she sees him seated in his living room, holding a book he isn't reading. She sees him hear the doorbell. She sees him wait. He turns a page of the book. She sees him make her wait.

'It's a question,' he says, when he finally comes, 'of the nature of the flood. We can investigate but will you like the outcome? There'll be costs to bear, Doctor Dover. More than if you sorted it yourself. More costs for you, person-ally, perhaps. It's you I'm considering. You'll appreciate we must know where the water's coming from. Outside in. Inside out. Human Error, Act of God. It tells us what house funds can be put forward. Procedures, Doctor. All in the interests of balance, of a smooth-running house.'

She takes a step away from him, a step down, like a sigh. She's still an inch taller. As he talks, the sun travels all over the top of his bare head, a bright blob squeezing about like an egg yolk. You can hear the high street one block on, mothers steering buggies towards the ample, antique park, and the call-centre staff on coffee runs, shuttling down from their multistorey office blocks, and the refuse workers knocking off and getting stoned, and the cascading shouts of morning breaktime at the local primary...

Above them, in the skies of the city, cranes moan and caw, magicking into the frosty air long ladders of one-room apartments to house those golden, jangling overseas students the empty-pocketed university is calling to, calling to... But it's quiet here, with Ivy and Cox-Coburn, on their meandering, no-through-road crescent of architecturally significant homes, where you know everyone's face and no one is *just passing through*...

'You'll have your position on the subject,' he says. 'You'll have your contractors in place. But it's only proper that I – which is to say "we", which is to say "the house" – it's only proper that *the house* makes an assessment to determine, objectively, so to speak – from the outside looking in, so to speak – the cause. Wouldn't you agree?'

She doesn't answer. He has a way of pausing that invites no response. He has a way of saying *Doctor Dover* that makes her feel like a child.

'Due process, Doctor Dover. You'll have thrown money at it already, seen what sticks. But if the house gets herself involved, well, we can't just pour our good money after bad, now, can we? Money rolls downhill, so to speak. Trickle-down, so to speak. Due process. I've seen what happens without due process. I've lived here a lot longer, remember. Seems like only yesterday you moved in. When you were a youngster. You and your young friends. No, it's the sort of thing that makes enemies of neighbours, this. Structural matters. The foundations. Best avoided. I certainly don't want to be your enemy...'

She finds a chance to interject. He's right, she says. The house. She agrees they should think of the house. She feels the same, how he feels about the house. So, she'll do as he advises. She'll bring in workers, take it forward on behalf of the house, keep the house updated.

'Don't trouble yourself,' says Cox-Coburn. 'Lucky for you, I've a professional connection, a pair of lads not otherwise engaged. Men who don't mind holiday work. My boys, I call them. The heavies! Hah! Getting the job done. Applying a little force. All without you even noticing. The rug out from under you, so to speak. Hah! Won't even know we're there.'

He must have practised it for years, this breezy pushiness. But she's a doctor. She deals in death and drugs. Why's she intimidated?

'A key?' he says. 'No need. As chair of the building, I have access already. The master. You know that, of course. Only for precautionary purposes. Very rare I would have entered your home. You wouldn't have known. Not a hair out of place. No, don't trouble yourself. We'll let ourselves in. Quiet as mice. Quiet as ghosts. You won't even know.'

They've had her here a decade, the neighbours, and in that time no owners have changed, so Ivy's still new, they all believe. The only other change of ownership was when the old man on the top floor died and was succeeded by his middle-aged son.

'It was my childhood home,' the son has said. 'Why leave where I was happiest? I still feel him in the rooms, as if he never left.' The son has never married, so he's still a son. Ivy's still a daughter. She remembers the old man up there. The son looks more like his father every day.

They've watched Ivy aging too, so how does she look to them now? They've known her since she moved in, witnessed her student days, the parties (one or two) and noise (not much of that), the failures to do her share for the building… They met Keele. They saw Keele around. They'd have registered Ally and Laine's departure. They would know about Keele's death, wouldn't they? No one ever said anything. Did she notify them? Where would his death fit in? Not a topic for Residents' Association meetings. No room for its bullet point on the agenda. They knew, at least, that she lived alone now, that she had lived with others but that she now, like they all did, lived alone.

'We like-minded ladies,' One-Two had said. 'We female professionals who live alone…'

Keele never played nice with the neighbours. Uncommunicative in the common spaces. Passive-aggressive about tenement rules. It got so bad, very early on, that they thought he was a trespasser… Ivy doesn't want to be that way. To accommodate your life, you have to get along with people. Good platitudes make good neighbours. If she says just enough, if she does just enough, she can get by. Swallow enough, too. Let Cox-Coburn be Cox-Coburn.

Sometimes, you need your neighbour, though you'd like it to be otherwise. After seeing Cox-Coburn, Ivy goes in at the main entrance and up to knock at One-Two. She hates to ask for help, but over the years she's walked One-Two's dog, watered One-Two's plants, offered second opinions on One-Two's medical concerns… so isn't she due?

She rarely comes into the central stairwell. There's no need. But, entering now, she's uplifted, coming into its expansiveness and spareness, the walls a rich red, the space opening upwards to the higher floors; uplifted, the staircase unfurling thinly, like curling paper, like an elegant, spiralling balcony, with this wrought-iron banister, with these broad and shallow steps, the gracefulness of which she can feel in her own footsteps, as she rises easily towards One-Two's door. Above her, the skylight draws together into a diamond-point and, passing through it, sunlight refracts and tilts, coming down to her in layers of gorgeous, impressionistic shadows. She likes it here. She's part of this. Even in the gloom of the basement flat, she can feel the house lifting and opening above her. It breathes. She hears that piano. A frost lies on the city. The city is as clear as ice. The Geologist is gone. Ivy lives in a house of neighbours, a neighbour of neighbours.

She knocks at One-Two.

Knock-knock.

The piano stops.

The last note thins in the air like an icicle.

She could ask someone else to feed the cat – Cox-Coburn, or the old son upstairs… But she likes One-Two, in a way. She hates and likes One-Two. She likes One-Two's lack of interest in her. One-Two won't ask questions about Ivy's set-up because it offers One-Two no intrigue. Also, One-Two is a woman. Ivy could do without any more men in her home.

'When would this be?' says One-Two. 'I might not be around.'

Well, perhaps Ivy can work around her. When isn't she available?

'I can't say exactly. What are your days?'

Ivy tells her some dates.

'Yes, that can't be guaranteed.'

Okay, no problem. No, it isn't a problem. Ivy can make other arrangements. But, out of friendly curiosity, what are One-Two's plans, this holiday season? Where will One-Two be while she's away?

'Away? No, I'll be spending Christmas at home.'

Ivy smiles. She must have made a misstep somewhere. She must have offended One-Two somehow, sometime. She lets it go, turns to go. She turns back.

By the way, Ivy says. I met your lodger.

Lodger? The word corks itself in her throat: lodged. *Lodger. Do we still use that word?* It sounds out of place – a square peg, a round hole – the whole idea of it.

I met your lodger. He seems nice. Is he?

Ivy, you're a dog with a bone. If you like him, all well and good. If you like him, fine. But why all this gnawing away at it? The right thing is to end it. But if that's the case, why don't you? Ivy, what's got into you? Ivy, I don't recognize you at all.

Your lodger. What was his name again? What did you say he does?

'Lodger?' says One-Two. 'What lodger? I don't have a lodger,' putting a little beat between every statement.

'I have *had* lodgers.' Is she being tricky? The trickiness, it's possible, isn't coming to Ivy from the outside-in, but travelling from the inside out. It's how she perceives it, how it enters her, passes through her, refracting, tilting.

Probably I'm confused. Maybe I'm thinking of someone previous. Or someone entirely unrelated! Different people come and go. Life's rich tapestry! A real spectrum! That's a good thing... And Ivy's definitely being tricky now, or clever, or just stirring the pot.

'A little too rich of a tapestry, perhaps,' says One-Two. 'Some evenings, it's as if the building has saloon doors. All these guests and girlfriends. All Rabbit's friends and relations. Quite the spectrum, you're right. Too many colours in the rainbow these days, don't you think?

'My lodgers, certainly,' One-Two continues, warming up, 'aren't all they should be, not all they purport. The last one up and vanished overnight. This was a number of days ago. A week or two, perhaps. Right when the rent was due! He was with me only a matter of months. Then suddenly he left. He claimed to be a scholar. Something at the university. It's why I took him in. Out of the storm, so to speak. Some scholar! A very raggedy gentleman. But I suppose you can be a scholar of anything these days. There are scholars and there are scholars. Lodgers? No, I don't recommend lodgers. I don't recommend taking in men. This man. Oversized. A grizzly, bearded, oversized man. Not a city type. Never much to say for himself.

Rarely hauled himself from his room. If I'm honest, a few days passed before I knew he'd gone...

'What's more, he never took a guest. Of which I approved, I must admit. Except once. One visitor, in all his weeks with me. Another odd fellow. Oddity loves company, I suppose. Looked dressed for a funeral. Behatted. Well, that was the one unquiet night. The opposite end of the scale. Opposite end of the Richter scale, you might say! Oohoohoo. Oh, I've amused myself there. Rather clever of me, in fact, given my tenement tenant's academic discipline, but I won't bore you. Anyway, what a commotion it was. Such shouting. A terribly unbecoming confrontation between the two of them, these two men. All in his room. Over and done with quickly. The visitor left almost straightaway. And the lodger must have moved out not long after.

'Then he was strange about the rent. Not what you think. He always paid on time. So particular about it. When he was here, he'd quibble over my house rules. But after he'd gone, he sent a letter paying double for the month and over-apologizing horribly. Hand-posted, too. No address, no stamp. I still see him around. The beard. The frown. The shuffle. I still see him, so he can't have gone far...

'And that letter! It said he'd found somewhere else. He said he was sorry because it wasn't my fault that we'd never got along, which I'd never considered until then. But I suppose it was true, yes, I didn't like him, and I suppose he was just being honest. I don't suppose it was his fault either. However, I do consider my manners exemplary, by today's standards – crisp and clear – and I pride myself that you wouldn't know, meeting me, if I rather liked you or if I despised you. Well, this chap said it couldn't be helped, his sudden departure, and it was out of his control but he'd fallen in love. Can you imagine? Love!'

18.

South. She is south. South of the border. All of it is south to the people of the city where she lives. Cross the border and you've gone south. But she is further south. Hours and hours south. South of city upon city. A southerner, back in the South.

On the drive from the station to their parents' cottage, Clover carries on about everything and nothing. No snow down here. Muddy. A warmth to the chill. They turn suddenly off the dual carriageway onto the brown, country lane that ends in the white cottage Ivy grew up in.

'Just so you're prepared,' says Clover, 'our bedrooms are now guestrooms. We're guests in our own home! Guests in our own bedrooms! They've had a whole upheaval. They've finally painted us out of the picture!'

There's been plenty of time to mention this already, instead of carrying on about Tiger and Him Indoors, so why say it now when they're nearly there? But why should it bother Ivy, anyway? Ridiculous to get upset about anything in that long-ago childhood. Nothing is upsetting in that childhood of loving loved ones.

'I'll admit I felt a little pang about it,' Clover says. 'My room! My things! But keeping shrines to your daughters is eery, right? Especially when they're still alive!'

They rumble up the track, over potholes their father still fills every summer, with the other men of the village.

'Bump-bump-bump,' says Clover. 'All these memories come jolting back. Like you and Iain up in your bedroom. Not a lot of noise. Just some creaking of the bedframe. But while you were up there, Dad would say, "What a racket! What are they doing? Rearranging the furniture?" when he must have known… "The ceiling's about to cave in!" he'd say, and meanwhile I'd sit there, avoiding all eye contact, mortified!'

In the porch, their mother ties long twigs with ribbon, wearing her old clothes for outdoor foraging and knocking about the house. Their father studies newspaper supplements, planning the season's television viewing. It always was a happy home. That isn't true of everyone. It isn't true of Keele, whose father upped and vanished when he was a child. She thinks it isn't true of the Geologist, either. She thinks he has a painful past. There's a brother, isn't there? A father. There's not much to go on.

'Him Indoors is upstairs, working on his masterpiece,' says Clover. 'Him *Upstairs*, I should say! Him Indoors is Him Upstairs when we're over for the holidays. Well, that's where he is. He'll stick his nose out sometime. He will! He's not that bad! He'll come down and be sociable. I'll make sure of it... Oh, Tiger, come and say hi to Aunty Doctor!'

If Ivy thought attention would be on her, she needn't have worried. Her parents are grandparents now. Everyone is freed from thinking of themselves, making not their own Christmas but a Christmas for the four-year-old. And here comes Tiger! Rushing along. With that not-quite-human character of a small child.

'Aunty Doctor! Let's play! You're playing with me! We're playing! Come! We're playing hospitals! We're playing doctors and nurses! You've hurt yourself! Badly! Tell me where it hurts! No, we're playing house! We're playing husbands and wives! We're married! No, owners and pets! No, daddies and children! You're the baby! You're having a lovely dream and I'm going to wake you up! You're crying! You're in tears!'

She remembers bringing Keele here. Petlike, springier than she is now, she sees herself pattering up these same stairs. He follows her. There's excitement in him, she can tell. And she's excited by it, a boy getting into her bedroom. He has found a way in, this boy, found a way to being invited. A Sunday. Her parents in the house.

In you come, Dream-Boy.

On the bed, this bed, she pats the space beside her. He won't sit.

'Looks like it's taken.'

What, her? Is he nervous about Nana? Why? Good old Nana! Memories of Keele bring that back, too. Memories of Nana. What a cat she was. As weighty as a sleeping dog. Nana. A hefty, fluffy tortoiseshell, bunched up fatly on top of the duvet. Nana. Like the actual shell of a giant tortoise.

Don't worry about her—

Then she scoops the cat up – she can feel it in her arms, even now – gathering the old lady, like pizza dough that keeps drooping from her hold, needing folding over again, dolloping back into itself. She can feel it. A lovely feeling, in her arms. A bucket of life, sloshing about.

But when Keele sits down... awful of her, she knows, but she suddenly throws Nana back to him. *What? Whoa!* He isn't ready. Doesn't even try to catch the thing. It wriggles to get away. Kicking. Landing on the carpet.

But Keele has jumped up again too! And now the cat's back on the bed. And he's left standing once more, no idea what to do with himself, sullenly watching the place he's lost. It's like Nana's his nemesis. It's like Nana's a door he can't open.

Ivy giggles. She wants this. This teasing. This wrestling. Boys and cats.

Not a cat person?

He doesn't answer. Has she hurt his pride?

Not a dog person, I hope?

He shakes his head.

'Cat person? Dog person? Nothing like that. I'm a poet.'

Okay, Mr Poet, did you bring your revision notes?

'Screw study. I'm a poet and I love you.'

She rolls her eyes.

Typical Dream-Boy.

She snuggles up with Nana on the bed.

See how cuddly? she says.

She wants the boy to think of cuddling her, this girl.

Then: Have I told you about Nana?

She's rubbing her thumb between the cat's eyes.

About Nana. Did I ever tell you how she got her name? I know it's stupid but I don't care. It was after my grandmother died. We bought Nana the next day and named her after my grandmother. *Nana.* My parents say it was my idea. I don't remember it like that. It was the cat's idea, as I remember it. That's not the whole story…

I was inconsolable about her. My grandmother. I can put myself right there. So final, when someone dies. Like a door closing. Goodbye, and the door closes. It locks. I couldn't accept it. I didn't really believe in death. Big feelings for a little girl. Do you have memories like that? Ones you can live inside? Maybe nothing's happened in my life so far, but there are memories… When I think of her dying, I feel it all over again.

There's not much before that. Not of Nana. Not of anything. Too young for anything to stick, I guess. Except that one thing. Except when she died. I don't remember her when she was alive. That's what doesn't make sense. I remember losing her, and how sad I was, but not her. And 'Nana the Cat' is old now. 'Nana the Grandmother' died years ago… I'll explain.

What it is. I've always believed that when she died, just before she died, my grandmother's soul lifted out of her body. Then it stayed and floated above our heads, while we were at the hospital, while we were driving home, while we slept in our beds… and didn't go anywhere until we drove to the cat-breeder's house. That's my second memory. Picking out a cat. It's when Nana's soul came down again and went inside this little, speckled kitten we chose.

Now Nana is Nana. I know her very well. But she's just *Nana*. I know she's my grandmother and I know she's a cat. But, because I don't remember my grandmother, who knows what parts are human and what parts cat? For example, was she always this cranky? Was she just as snoozy, as a woman? It's bound to change you, turning into a cat. Can you imagine!

'A talent of mine,' says the boy. 'An overactive imagination.'

I said a prayer, she continues. I may as well tell you everything. I said a prayer. I took to the hospital the book she would read me. I couldn't read yet, but I read it to her. I knew it off by heart. I didn't know any prayers, but I read her that book, in front of Mum and Dad and the nurse and my sister, Clover, who was even younger than I was.

Only a children's book, but I know I was saying a prayer. A story about a child inviting a giant creature into their home from outside. Something from jungles and dark places. And their home becomes as strange as those outside places, becomes magical... And, yes, I'm going to be a doctor, but can't doctors believe in magic? What's more magic than science? You're a poet, so you must believe in magic words.

Look, I know it's impossible, but that's how my grandmother died and became a cat. And it's how I chose to become a doctor. It's impossible, but that doesn't matter. What's the difference now? Whatever's grandmother, whatever's cat, she's all Nana. Now she's an old lady again, aren't you, my darling? So, she's in her element.

You think I'm mad, don't you?

He speaks.

'May I stroke your grandmother?' he says.

She's smiling.

Don't ask me. Ask her.

They're all smiling, all three. Grinning like cats.

And the boy reaches out. He holds Nana's paw.

'Nana,' he says. 'May I ask for your granddaughter's hand in marriage?'

The cat's unimpressed. But not Ivy. She falls about laughing.

Okay, okay, marriage. No problem. But first, homework. First, school.

19.

Empty flat. Sunlight moving differently. Time losing shape. Time pooling, blooming, creeping, trickling, coming and going, never staying in place. He's alone. She's left him. It was only a matter of time. He waits for her. Only a matter of time. He stays, sleeps, watches, waits…

If he wakes, it's a dreaming wakefulness. If he dreams, it's a waking dream. He moves like sun and shadow on the walls. Not so tied to time. Not so tangled in time. The way he moves, he holds time at the edge of his vision, a prey, a pulsing mouse… Sleeping and dreaming and watching and wanting. And hoping, despairing, moaning, mewing.

A cat meowing in a forest, does he make a sound?

No one enters.

If anyone enters, he can hide. You won't catch him. Not even the flick of his tail. He's scarce. A disappearing act. A disappearing cat. Making himself scarce. Making himself scared.

Someone enters.

A new sound enters. A different cranking in the lock. Then into the kitchen steps the bald man. The beaming bald head: the bald man, coming in, confidently. Proprietorial, predatory. Looking like the new homeowner he maybe is.

Retreat. Keep your distance. Don't be found. Watch him walking around unawares, as if unobserved, inspecting here and there, giving little taps and raps and slaps, and saying nothing. Voicing no thoughts. Thinking nothing. Nothing inside the man. And nothing inside Berry. No words. No humans in the room. Only these two empty creatures...

How good to be a cat! How good to be a nothingness! How good, watching people when they're alone. More intimate than anything they'll ever know. Seeing everything in them, every human detail, every human breath.

It makes you love what living is. But then you start to come alive. You start to live a little more, being around these living people. Too lovely, you long for more life, for a human life, however stupid, however difficult, to live in human difficulty, in human desire...

The door closes.

He checks for changes. The cleared-up litter tray. The fresh food in the bowl: a new, dry dinner. *Dispose of it*. That's necessary. Anytime the bald man enters, Berry clears away the food. But there's no hunger. Even days the bald man doesn't come, he has no hunger. The impulse is gone. No catlike cravings. He's nothing. Not a cat. Not a memory. Not dead. Not alive. He's hers. All he knows is how to wait, how to want...

Something else. Here.

Not her. Not the big man. Not the bald man. Something else, in the kitchen. Almost in the kitchen. Nearby. Test the room. Test every corner. Tilt your ears. Put out feelers. Nothing. Nobody. Then: there! In the cat-flap window. The face of the neighbour cat, watching.

Afterwards, it's gone. But when did it go? Gone, but he keeps seeing it, cross-hatched behind the scratched-up little screen... A beautiful, placid face. Dead-eyed desire. Bronze-brown-yellow-white-wheat-coloured... and turquoise eyes like wren's eggs in a nest.

Something else.

Another something. The neighbour cat gone. Gone hours or days or seconds ago. Gone, but something else here. Night. Day, a moment ago. It was day, days ago. Now there's something at the dark window... there.

A head in a black hat. A new stranger. Empty face under a black hat, peering through the window, the eyes moving in the head, searching all over the room, searching over different areas of darkness, over the black cat in the black darkness.

Then that's gone, too. And he can't recall a single feature. Maybe it had no features at all. No mouth, no eyes. Without a nose. He didn't see it as a face. He felt it. The stranger. The strange creature. Known to him, somehow. When it went, the face drew away like a curtain. The black hat had withdrawn, taking the face with it. He knows what it was.

That's it, he thinks.

That's the third being.

The nemesis.

The one to kill the mountain man.

20.

In the old childhood room, her bed is in a different place. Not her room but, yes, it is the room of someone she once was. Already, she feels a mewing pining for the tenement in the north, for those empty rooms with little Berry moving through them. How's the flat? How's the cat? How's Berry coping with Cox-Coburn stopping by each day to fill his bowl?

Was that the right decision, Ivy, welcoming Mr Duplex's kind offer? Why won't it sit right with me, the thought of Cox-Coburn letting himself into my home?

On the childhood bed, the sheets are now white and patterned with small scribbly trees and birds, the same pattern on one wallpapered wall. Why is it that the smell of fresh paint calms her? She thinks of Keele and Nana on the bed. Crisp, white sheets, without the slightest impression upon them. These sheets, they make the cat and boy more alive and more dead both.

Putting down her bag, she sees the cardboard box marked 'Ivy's Remnants!' and the note saying, 'Keep What Want. Rest For Charity. Love Mum/Dad.' She kneels. Across the little square landing she can see her parents' closed door and Clover's closed door. She hears her brother-in-law shifting about. That man! *Him Indoors*. He must bring something to the equation. Clover insists he's a good man. But he's been working on 'his masterpiece' for years and Ivy hasn't seen sign of it. There's never that much parenting, either.

In the box are familiar and unfamiliar things. It must all be hers. It must be something to do with her. She puts everything into the 'Charity' pile. Then she picks up the bundle of Keele's letters and poetry. Keele's writings.

Always hard to say what was a poem, what was a letter. You'd have thought the line breaks and rhymes would be a clue. Surprising how often she couldn't tell. But he wouldn't have liked her saying that. 'There's not a word out of place, Ivy! Can't you see what it is? It's exactly what it is!' Thumbing through a notebook, she lands on her favourite poem.

'If I Was Your Cat'

All day, she wants to be back in the bedroom. But after a dinner of many parts, prepared by Clover and their mother, when Ivy says goodnight to everyone, Clover will say, 'How about a game?' Then she'll call to Him Indoors, as well, up in their room where he's been putting Tiger to bed, but he always turns her down.

'Just family, then,' Clover says. 'This family, I mean. Hold it right there, Sis. You're not getting away that easily. You're not going anywhere,' spreading her fingers over the scattered diamonds, spades, hearts, clubs, to keep Ivy and herself and their parents in place.

'Who doesn't like playing cards?!' Clover would say to Keele, when they were young, the three of them, Clover, Keele and Ivy, at this same table.

Then Keele would answer, 'It's not for me. A words guy, not a numbers guy. I like real life, not games. I'm not like you, Lucky. I'm not a game-player.'

In the end, after a few too many rounds, nearing midnight, when Ivy can retreat, can get herself to bed, she looks again at Keele's poem. She doesn't need the written thing. She remembers every word. She's read it many times before. Alone now in her old room, holding it in her hands, she recites it again under her breath, eyes opening, eyes closing.

In this bed. With Keele. In this same bed. They would lie whispering. Why whisper? What did it matter? Ivy's sister was the only other person in the house. No, it didn't matter. But they were whispering in one another's ears. He talked about poems, his future and ambitious dreams. She talked about medicine, her childhood and private shames.

'One day,' he said, 'I'll leave this small world, this small country, and wander the planet, without a plan, without a place. Place to place. Living in the moment. Everything will be a new discovery you can't name. I'll just, just, just... be. Beyond words. Strange landscapes...'

Meanwhile, her hands, unseeing, ventured over parts of him.

I want to admit something else about Nana, she said.

Why say that? But she said it. I want to admit something...

He didn't answer. In the dark, she looked for where his voice would be.

It's something I'm ashamed of, she told him. But I want to tell you. I don't know why I want to tell you, but I do.

Then, when she said the thing, he still said nothing. She didn't think he was asleep. It was the worst answer, saying nothing at all. What did he think of it? The thing she'd told him. The image of her. A younger girl. Much younger. Thirteen years old. Nana in her lap. That shameful admittance. Her Nana in her lap. Her grandmother cat... But still he said nothing.

Then she knew he hadn't been asleep because now each of his limbs trembled, juddered and lay quiet, and he really was sleeping. Beside him, she stayed wide awake. *Don't ever say a word about anything,* she reminded herself.

The next day, he stayed with her in the quiet cottage, and neither of them talked again about the story she'd told. But, by the evening, he'd written the new poem, 'If I Was Your Cat'.

Then, more than a year later, he came to the garden door of her flat, and she let him in and he came through her kitchen, past Ally, past Laine, through her hallway, into her bedroom. She took him inside. They made love. She slept. But he woke her again. He was restless, he said. He wanted to talk about the Nana stories: the first, about Nana being Nana; and the other, the second Nana story.

'Ivy, you're everything.' It was hard to focus on him: she wasn't quite awake. She didn't know where she was. It was night. What time was it? 'What it means. That Nana story. I want you to know what it means…' It was Ivy's story, not his, but maybe she didn't understand it. He wanted her to understand it. The meaning had to be voiced. If she couldn't, he would. Maybe it embarrassed her, but she was wrong about that.

He began to describe it all over again, what she'd told him. About the thirteen-year-old girl. About the lady cat in her lap. About the grandmother cat in her lap. The warm purrs in her lap. The warm purrs growing warmer and stronger, until they grew through her. Until they grew peculiar. Until they grew up through her like a flower. Until they came from inside the girl herself. Warm purrs growing. Warm purrs grew. A yawning, weepy feeling, rising and rising inside. Cat purring in her lap. Cat warming her. Cat trembling. The feeling rising. Growing. Growing unbearable. Until it broke like a storm, rattling shutters, bringing down tiles, blowing open doors.

Awfully. Incredibly. Caused by her pet cat. Caused by her dead grandmother. She was ashamed.

'But it's wonderful,' he said. Did she see how wonderful it was? Her body, her memories, her sensations, her movements, her innocence… He couldn't look away. He had to give it words. Maybe she didn't see it, so he had to speak for her. A parade of words. Downpour of words.

She was awake now. She was trying to sleep. She turned away from him. She rolled over and turned away. She knew he was aroused. He was desperate. Those two Nana stories she had told, they were tangled like tails inside him, messing him up.

No, she answered, that's not important, that story about Nana. I probably overplayed that. It probably didn't happen like that. I'm not sure it was even true. I was trying to be interesting. I was a teenager. I still am, I know, but nearly not, and not really. I was a schoolgirl, trying to impress you. I don't think that way about masturbation anymore. The cat was always just a cat. We were at school when I said that. It was over a year ago. I was a child. I was childish. I was preposterous. Obviously, Nana wasn't ever actually my grandmother. Dead now, anyway.

21.

It's a long break from the Southern Royal. At work, they reminded her that using up a certain amount of leave was a legal requirement. And overtime did, in fact, accrue more leave. Overtime did not, as she might have hoped, eat away at what leave she had. A job was not a holiday. The hospital would always find work for you. The hospital was crying out for warm bodies. Especially at Christmas. But Ivy never took leave at Christmas. She was firmly encouraged to take it now...

So, she's with her family for days. And each day in the cottage proceeds the same way, with games and walks and too many meals together. Sometimes, Ivy gets herself away. She takes her phone into the woods. She doesn't message the Geologist. The Geologist doesn't message.

These woods. She knows them so well she can get lost on purpose. *Ivy, you're going around in circles.* Real streams run through it. Pools of bluebells in spring. Mud. Passageways of brown, twining trees. Huge hollow stumps like entranceways to other worlds. She knows it all… Fungi in yellow, cakey wedges. Fungi like miniscule white sconces, each cap a tiny, translucent lampshade. Fungi like crinkly oysters.

A large man, one summer, baring himself to them, her and her sister… That fear of oversized men, it stayed with her.

She thinks of the Geologist, in these woods, or in her childhood home, too large for the low-ceilinged cottage, too large for a girl's single bed, for her child-sized memories. It makes no sense. *Oddity loves company.* He could be anyone.

She thinks of that other stranger at the hospital, too, the Plain Clothes, the man with the hat. She thought she saw him again once. Not at the hospital, but around the neighbourhood. She was walking home to the flat, thinking of the Geologist waiting there, when she saw him. A man in a hat.

It can't have been him. He was pasted against a wall like a shadow. He was outside that restaurant called Hops & Heron, with its front of artfully crisping old paint and a preserved ghost sign reading '*Tobacco & Ice Cream*'. As she approached, he peeled off, turned out of sight. Probably it wasn't him. Just another hatted man. Men do wear hats, don't they?

She feels thronged by them, the strange men of the city. She's glad to get away, to wander these trees. But it's evening now. She turns back towards home.

Opening the door, she hears her mother calling. 'Dinner's on the table for those who want it! And for those who don't!'

Even after dinner, even then, when Ivy can get to her bedroom, she isn't done. Clover comes in and sits on her bed. Ivy's under the duvet but Clover witters away in a sisterly mode, as if they've always talked like this, as children and young women. Clover sits there, cute. A small, womanly body. A girl. Why come in here? Isn't she eager to get back to Him Indoors? To share these talky thoughts with him instead? Clover's own little room is crowded with a bedded-down husband and a sleeping child.

'I'll have to spend an age edging around them before finding a space to sleep in,' she says. 'But what about you, Sis? Something's up, isn't it? I can tell. There's a secret you're keeping. I can read you like a book. Always could. What you don't know is it's a romance novel. Give me something. A titbit. Half a chapter before bed. If you talk, I'll listen. You should hear that I care. So much gets in the way, especially when you're family. But you should hear that I care. Don't let *me* get in the way. Don't let *you* get in the way…'

Afterwards, Ivy lies alone, awake, and starts to tell herself Keele's poem – *If I was… If I was…* – until other words slip in. Now she's hearing the Geologist's list for knowing stones. She hadn't meant to think of him but now they're at the table together in her night-time kitchen, with candles lit and blue snow outside. And he's explaining for her the science of stones. Geologists have a system of tests, he's telling her, for categorizing rock. How easy for you lot! she laughs. All you need to do is go by what you can see, what you can touch…

'A series of checks,' he's saying. 'For example, we check for *lustre*. It means the quality of light when you look.'

And he meets her eyes.

He's holding her small hand in his big hands. And their hands aren't the same species. She can't recognize her own hand, in his hand, in the night kitchen, in this candlelight and streetlight and moonlight and snowlight. He's holding her hand. He's tracing the lines of her palm. He's looking closely at her fingers.

'We test for magnetism,' he says.

And he places her hand on his giant chest.

'We test for effervescence,' he says.

And, honestly, her heart is fizzing.

Lustre.

Magnetism.

Effervescence.

The Geologist's poem.

She recites it into sleep.
Hardness.
Breakage.
Gravity.
She's dreaming.

Another night, Clover goes upstairs before her. Ivy's in the living room with their mother and father. There are noises above. It's Clover and the husband arguing. Ivy sits there, avoiding all eye contact. She remembers what Clover had said. *You and Iain. Up in your room. Creaking of the bedframe. Rearranging furniture.*

Tiger's in that room, too. He'll sleep through anything, it seems. Looking at the ceiling, Ivy notices an unrelated hairline crack. You can't hear what they're saying. Sometimes, the muffled talking breaks out in a strongly spoken word, short, curt, almost recognizable, an axe-like chop.

Mostly, it's Clover speaking. A voice that's high and frail and won't let up. Cheery even when desperate. She sounds like a search party, calling into a maze of caverns. The husband's lost somewhere in there. *Listen to my voice! I'll find you!* Sometimes, she'll pause, opening a silence into which Him Indoors says nothing.

Or, if he does speak, it's just one or two low syllables. He sounds like a voice in the wall. He sounds far away, as if he's in another room to her, though they're together.

Honestly, it's how he always sounds, even when you're face to face with him. A slow, below-ground voice. A voice pulled up, unwillingly, from the depths of him.

'A passionate pair,' says Ivy's father.

22.

In lulls in the cottage, she finds she's looking forwards to him, the Geologist. In lulls, she's thinking of a day they left the flat and walked down through the city, to stroll along the river. They bought ice-creams from a newsagent's. In winter! Such nonconformists! Such iconoclasts! The whole riverwalk was frozen over treacherously.

Why do I always slip up around you? she said.

He liked that.

The river surface had a glassy, misty film. When the Geologist looked downriver, Ivy felt he was looking further than she could see, out to the firth, the estuary, the opening into bays, sounds, isles, peninsulas… into shoals, spits, sandbanks, sandbars… into the ocean. She thought he was thinking of a vast geography of islands, of a vast history of landscape. He was talking again about rocks, this time about 'scholar stones'.

But I don't care in the slightest about bloody rocks, she thought. *So why do I so love to listen?* And she licked at her chocolate cone. And about scholar stones he held forth, about the art of stone appreciation. For thousands of years, he said. The aesthetic contemplation of stones. Ivy couldn't help laughing. *Stones!* But she remembers all the criteria of appreciation.

Slenderness.

Texture.

Glossiness.

The sound.

The sound! Of a rock! What's the sound of a rock? *Thud?!*

'A lot like the scientific criteria,' the Geologist said. 'Lustre. Magnetism. Effervescence. Brittleness, how it breaks up... Course, some profs don't call geology a science. Not scientific enough. But some say that about most of the sciences. And if you go back far enough, back to scholar stones, art and science, it all gets very amorphous, very porous.'

Amorphous? Porous? Aesthetics? What was he? Was he the strong, silent type? Or was he something bright and bubbly and buoyant? He was a river. Maybe Ivy was the silent, solitary stone, not him. She was a strange specimen he'd dug up.

They finished their ice-creams and were about to turn back the way they'd come. She hugged his big arm and said, Let's go home. Then she said that she'd like to buy him a scholar stone for his birthday. But the best, he'd told her, were worth tens of thousands, so Ivy said, Well, if I was a millionaire then. You could study it. You could get to know it…

'Ta, but never wanted to own anything. Not a house. Not a person. Not a stone. Wouldn't want to hold it back.'

It's a stone. It isn't going anywhere.

'Not today,' was his answer. 'Not tomorrow. But even stones roll. Even stones slip, fall, tumble. Never wanted to stand in anything's way. Want to let things be. Let everything be. Moreso, what I love the most. Enough to know it's there.'

Texture, she told herself, walking with him by the river.

Glossiness.

Slenderness.

Sound.

The river kept slowly flowing away.

Boxing day. A Residents' Association email.

Dear all,

Confirmation of house payment for Minus One-One flooding authorized. Identified cause: uncapped spout on downpipe. Therefore: Wastewater of Two-One, One-One and Zero-One detouring through Minus One-One's interior. Utilization of house funds assessed, accepted and approved.

Signed off.

C-C (Residents' Association Chair)

PS. Let's hope that's an end to it. No further damages sought for alleged delays by the Residents' Association. No further damages sought against Two-One, One-One, Zero-One or otherwise, being obviously not liable for their wastewater overflowing and pouring into Minus One-One. No 'gushing apology' needed, let's hope. No more trouble at your end, Minus One-One, let's hope. No more surprises! All well and as it should be with the house.

PPS. Because I can't keep sending in men on a whim. So, no more disturbances, please. In the foreseeable... because it was a concern, to the house. Don't think it wasn't. We did share concerns. Concerns were shared in meetings. Don't think we weren't aware, Doctor Dover. Don't think we ignored the goings on 'down below'. A subject of discussion in the most recent of our meetings.

Ivy should leave it alone. The matter is dealt with. The flood is over and done with. Men are fixing down floorboards right this moment. But that comment about meetings... What meeting?

She replies to Cox-Coburn. Did she miss a meeting of the Residents' Association?

Miscommunication! he answers. *Not Residents' Association. Meetings of the board, I meant to say. For board meetings, not all are required. The Chair. The Treasurer.*

Certain vested parties. Your various issues were discussed, don't worry. One-Two, in particular, stated a number of issues in connection to you, on your behalf…

The board? She's never heard of a residents' board. So, there are additional board meetings? But the entire building is only seven separate homes. Since when have these extra meetings been going on?

Five minutes later, another email arrives:

Actually, Minus One-One, Cox-Coburn says, *now that I have you, I wanted to raise…*

She almost feels his presence, almost feels him take a step towards her, as she reads his words. *Now that I have you. Your floors. My men can do more. Not only the spare room. We needn't stop there. Initial inquiries do tend to unearth… How can I put this? Once you start turning over rocks, Doctor Dover… Once you start pulling at threads… Now that I have you, the whole floor is due a redo. The whole square footage. Wouldn't you agree? Then there are the walls, the plaster, the ceiling, too, now that I have you. The wiring. I flicked a few switches. On. Off. Nothing. Now that I have you, the wiring is a terrible spider's web. A death-trap. It does grow arms and legs, once you start looking…*

Then you consider Zero-One, above you. Arms and legs, as I say. But nothing to fear from all those arms and legs, my dear! My men can deal with all of it. Did the same with mine. Your rooms would be like finishing the job. Now that I have you, I'm sure we could come to an arrangement. Another duplex is doable. You're an independent unit, of course. You're independent from Zero-One, so that's a difference, at least for the time being. But who knows what the future holds? In this chaotic climate. I'm sure we can come to an arrangement. At a certain point, it's the whole house we're thinking of. Think what's best for the house. You won't be here forever.

She opens her mouth. Even only reading, she opens her mouth as if to answer, as if in protest. But she can't interrupt him. He won't be interrupted. She's still reading.

You won't, Minus One-One. You won't be here forever. Neither will I. But I'm set in my ways. I'm too invested. A duplex, after all. I don't see me leaving. If anything, I'll be more bedded down, more dug in. Bury me under the floorboards, they will! But not you, Doctor. You'll be off living your life. You've thought about that, haven't you? Selling. A shrewd move. In this dynamic climate. Your flat could really be something. A 'destination home'. You'll come to me first, won't you, when you decide?

C-C

She replies again. She shouldn't. She can't help herself.
Selling? No, you're stuck with me, I'm afraid!

His response is immediate.

167

Take my advice. Get it all looked at.
Sooner rather than later.
Those electrics, Ivy. Something's wired up wrong.
Watch it doesn't blow up in your face.
Watch out you're not sorry. I've seen it happen.

23.

Lying in the hall. Body along the wall. Head in the doorway. Unmoving. Watching the floor. Maybe sleeping. Warm. Warmth coming up through the floor. Warmth running under the floor. A warm pipe under the floor. A warm rod seeming to run through him, tongue to throat to tail. Did he choose here? One of his spots? One of Berry's spots? Lying here. Legs and long body along the wall, head in the doorway, watching the kitchen floor, the dim tiles, sunlight doodling about, insects scurrying…

What is it? Try to name it. What was it? There was a name. A name was there. Tip of the tongue. Yawning. Warm. Fading. But a face was there, a woman's face. Angled away. Seen from below. Steep. Vertiginous. The shins, knees, leaning torso, chin, the eyelids, looking away. Can't see her straight-on. Face to face. The mouth winking. The eyes making eyes. The face won't appear. The face with a name. The face named…

Black-legged, wire-thick, leg by leg by leg the spider comes closer on the kitchen tiles, large on the kitchen tiles and, snip-step-snip, every step is a snippet of time, and the name, the name is almost there, her name – Ivv-Ivv-Ivv – very nearly sounding itself aloud in the mouth, teeth, tongue, the special vocal cords very nearly speaking her name as, finger by finger by finger the spider— He bites! Snaps, and has it in his mouth. Crunching and kicking. A lively, black-lettered word.

The door opens.

'Through here. You're alright. Nobody home. This way, chaps.'

Up now. Standing. Hide. Watch the bald man, as he enters. Two more following in. Men, coming through the kitchen. The bald man, touching everything, the table, counter, walls, doors, doorframes, grabbing at the house like it's gingerbread, like it ought to break off in his hands.

Hide. Slip aside. Skip out of the way. As the bald man comes into the hall. Take cover. Take to this corner. Dip, slip, slink out the way. As the bald man reaches out, reaches down, reaches… Then he's taken hold. He's holding it, the small, framed picture of Iain Keele, gesturing with it, waving it at the others, tipping it up like an empty cup.

'She lives alone.'

The men grunt agreement.

He puts the picture down.

Then: 'Good God!' – squinting with his nose. 'Smell that?'

Then: 'A bombsite!' – arriving in the spare room.

And: 'What rot! Smells animal.'

And the bald man has animal in him. Berry senses it. Animal sensing animal. Takes one to know one. The bald man's eyes. The bald man's jaw. The doglike draw from snout to scalp. The man is ready to pounce. Ready to clamp teeth. Ready. Waiting. Wanting provocation.

'Gag,' says the bald man. 'Gag.'

He steps back.

'Have at it, gents,' – turning away.

But he doesn't go, not yet.

He looks around, gives other rooms the once-over.

'Big job,' he says quietly, talking to himself not the men. 'A real project. All this will come out. And this. And this. This, too. Out, out.'

He thumps at a wall.

'Non-supporting. Down it comes. Redone. Replaced. Gutted... Where's that puss got to? Puss. Puss. A lick of paint. Pussy-Puss-Puss. A lick. An undertaking. A lick of paint won't scratch the surface...'

Finally, he's going. So, follow him. Follow him out. Follow like you're his shadow. Drip, slip, trickle like a shadow. To the back door, but no further. Stop at the back door, but make sure he leaves. Watch him crossing the garden, till he's gone. Set not a paw outside, not yet. It's coming, but not yet. Not yet, but the door is open.

24.

On New Year's Eve, especially on New Year's Eve, Clover insists on mirth and warmth. Tiger's put to bed but will be woken – so they plan – a few minutes before midnight, to see in the new, see out the old. Who's that for? What resolutions could Tiger possibly have, what regrets? What would Tiger know about the past and the future?

Tonight, especially tonight, Him Indoors is keeping upstairs, too.

He does exist, doesn't he, this husband of yours? Ivy says.

Then Clover says, 'Stop taking the piss. Stop hating him for one minute. He's my husband. This is my husband, whatever anyone else thinks of him, however it looks to anyone else, whether or not it looks like happiness, by anyone else's standards.'

Ivy's immediately sorry and says so. I really was out of line, she says. After all, I can hardly criticize someone who just wants to be left alone. I don't blame him. I don't mind. Let him stay up there for all I care. It's just that I thought we were joking. I thought it was something we do. You used to joke about Iain, didn't you?

'Iain was different,' says Clover. 'Iain gave as good as he got. Iain was in on it. We were all joking together. It's not the same. My husband never did anything to anyone. He never does anything at all.'

Clover says that maybe she'll just go to bed.

And Ivy says, No, stay. Stay down here with us. It's New Year's Eve, says Ivy, surprised to be the one insisting it all mean something.

'Don't worry,' Clover answers. 'I'm just tired. It's been a long year. But happy new year, everyone! Let me know how it turns out. Goodnight, Mum and Dad. Goodnight, Sis.'

Then she's gone and Ivy looks at her mother who's looking at her.

What, Mum?

Her mother looks weary. Normally, she'd be in bed sooner. She sighs with her whole body. Ivy sees herself in her, as if her mother is the child. It's Ivy's solemnity but without the same meanness. Her mother conveys a parent's exhaustion, but no one needs her strained attentiveness anymore. Ivy got her height from her; now the woman's bones, in the order of things, are shrinking. She's a tall woman no longer tall.

'Ivy. Do you have to?' says her mother. 'You're not the same. The two of you. I've always known that and never treated you the same. I treated you fairly, but not the same. You know what she's like. She just believes in staying positive. She believes in making the best of things. That can be a strength, too. But you know what she's like. Always cried at her own birthday parties. Do you have to burst her balloon? Sadness doesn't come so easily to everybody, sweetheart.'

Ivy stands. She puts a hand on her mother's shoulder, rubs her mother's back. She chooses what of what her mother says will catch on her, what will go floating by. Yes, it's true she could be a better sister.

I'll talk to her, Mum. But she's probably gone to sleep.

She hasn't. She's in Ivy's room. When Ivy gets upstairs, she finds her there, in her bed.

'We're divorcing,' Clover says.

Divorce? Who's divorcing? At first, Ivy can't understand the statement. Can't hear it right. She runs through all the possibilities of divorce. Is this about their parents? She remembers those unfounded childhood fears, their sisterly debates together in this same bed. Oh, so they did talk sometimes, little Clover and Ivy. *Will it happen to us?* they'd wondered. *Divorce.* It had happened to another girl at school, and Clover had hugged the child, then been inconsolable with fears she'd brought the

curse home. Or is 'we' Ivy and Clover? *We're divorcing.*
We're no longer sisters. Has Ivy finally been such a bad
friend to Clover that her sister wants to call it quits?
Perhaps Ivy always seems to want nothing to do with
her, too distant. Is Clover calling her out on it, forcing
her hand?

No, she's divorcing her husband, Him Indoors.

Divorcing? says Ivy. No, you're not. You love each
other. You're happy. He's your husband.

Why's Ivy so insistent tonight? *He's your husband!*
It's New Year's Eve! Her brain simply can't process it
somehow. She can't imagine Clover unhappy. Unhappily
married. What was Clover like before she was a wife and
mother? Ivy can't see Him Indoors as a separate indi-
vidual, either, not quite a complete, convincing human.

'Not happy, no,' says Clover. 'Not in love. It isn't
working. I don't know if it ever was. I'm not sure it was
ever love. I don't know if I was ever sure. Sometimes,
I think that what I always thought was love was really
'worry'. And the feeling of being comfortable was actually 'melancholy'. It never came naturally to me. I can't
love like you. I couldn't fall in love with someone so
simply as you did with Iain.'

With Iain?

'Maybe I thought he was like Iain. His seriousness. His
frowns. The things he says, I always thought he was
joking. Now I'm not sure. There's a darkness to him.

There's bitterness. Disappointment. Maybe I thought he was romantic, like Iain was romantic with you. But shouldn't happiness just look like happiness?

'No, it's me. I know it's me. I want too much from him. He never said he was anything other than he is. He just says, "I am what I am. All there is to it." Last night he asked me why he should change when he'd never lied to me about who he was. Mostly, he says nothing at all. Meanwhile, I've been able to imagine he's a whole different person on the inside!'

Ivy sits on the bed. Clover rolls up against her.

'Remember how much Iain loved you? I've never known something like that. Remember how he'd look at you? Wowed. Like he didn't know what he was looking at. That summer. That summer you were about to leave, about to start becoming a doctor. That summer you were always in the garden, in the sunshine. His head would be in your lap, looking up at you. Like you were the sky. This smile on his face. Blissful. Like he was floating...'

Sometimes, Clover seems to be drifting off.

When she speaks again, she's somewhere else.

'I loved him, too. I know it's not right to say. I have no right. When he died... No, I didn't lose anyone. Not like you. But I loved him. I... it was like a brother, or something, I don't know. I loved him like a brother is what I think I mean. I loved him. He could be so... so...

'It was like being let in on something, being around you two. There were days, that summer, Mum and Dad out the house, there were days we felt like a little family, us three, you and Iain and me, how it felt to me, like we were grown-ups, or you were the married couple and I was the baby. It was love, how I felt.'

Sometimes Clover pauses. Sometimes she hurries on. She seems to be travelling through somewhere, lost, making turns, finding her way.

'I looked up to you, Ivy. You seemed so far ahead. Only a couple of years, but you seemed so far on, so far away. I didn't know anything about anything. I felt like an idiot. I was jealous. What of? Maybe I was jealous of you. Maybe it's that I was jealous of him because I'd lost you to him. I could hate him. Do you think that's when we stopped being so close? We were close once, weren't we?

'I would hang around you two. Remember? Just to be near you. And one time he said, "Why don't you join us?" but when I started coming over, he went, "Actually, Lucky, while you're up... are there beers in the house?" He was kind of a tease, wasn't he?

'Well, I went in and I came back out with two of Dad's beers. I wasn't going to drink anything, of course. I joined you on the grass. But you got up not long after. I remember exactly. You said, "I have to study. The bones won't memorize themselves. But you two stay." So, it was just

Iain and me, both sort of lying down. Sort of side by side. He was drinking the beer that had been for you.

'The sun was really hot. Really high. And Nana was sleeping in the shade of the holly tree. And Iain was planning a love poem for you, experimenting with all these words and rhymes out loud. It was the poem about if he was your pet cat. I came up with one or two lines, as well. I think he took some of my suggestions. He said it had to be like a vow. So, I came up with the "as we forgive those who trespass against us" bit.

'He visited once or twice that year when you were already at university. I thought it would feel nice, but it didn't. I didn't tell you that. I guess he told you that. I couldn't figure him out. Was it like that for you? He was so... Every way he behaved, he was so... confusing... I was so excited about his visit, but then... it felt wrong... it didn't feel right... it wasn't right...'

Then Clover's asleep. Sleeping. She has talked herself out, emptied herself out. She lies now, breathing gently, against Ivy's arm. It has a precise weight, this head. It's a spiralled shell. The sea-sound pours out of it like water. What is it about the weights of heads? It's profound to Ivy, her thoughts about all of their heads. Then suddenly it's macabre.

She switches off the lamp and closes her eyes. She recites Keele's poem. She recites the Geologist's test. It's midnight. It's a minute past.

Downstairs, there's the suck and smack of the fridge door, and the soundless easing free of the cork, and the tapping together of the two champagne glasses, their parents' quiet observance.

25.

The open door.

And Berry.

And the snow.

Next: the workmen. Coming and going. Their boots. All day. Days and days. The next day, the next day, day on day. Emptying out. Tipping out. The room emptying. Debris from the room pouring into the garden. As they dig out the hole inside. Hammering. Levering. Cracking. Splintering. Radio noise. Male voices singing like wounded animals. The hole grows. The whole hole. A human thought makes its way in. The old riddle:

The more you take away, the bigger I become.

What am I?

He tries something more. He tries another thought. But can't. Nothing arrives. So, he waits. He watches the outside. White and empty. Chilly and clear. Pieces of black, rotted wood amassing, piling on top of the slippery crust of ice that's covered the garden for weeks. And next: new planks are laid out. Crisp. Yellow. Like pineapple flesh. Ready to be brought in.

But still he waits. At the open door. At the often open door. He could leave any moment. But it's not the moment. It's almost the moment. Almost his moment. He waits. Watching the door. Watching the garden. Then snow begins. Snow. For the first time in days. A dry, dusty falling of snow.

Beginning, now melting into the slimy ice. Beginning, now settling onto itself. Beginning, now coming down more heavily. Heavier still. Beginning and beginning and beginning being borne down. Emptied out. Tipped out. The sky emptying. Debris from the sky pouring into the garden. Sackfuls of grey feathers descending in wide, corkscrewing columns. It's time.

It's here. He's here.

A mountainous, dark figure is coming through the white.

26.

New Year's Day, Ivy travels north. In the night, she has slept only a little. On the drive to the station, Clover hardly says a word. They lay all night together, and Clover slept deeply, unburdened, but now she's silent. Ivy never thought she'd long for Clover's talk. But for Ivy, nothing is wrong. For Clover, everything is wrong, it seems.

What had Clover said about Keele? That she loved him? That she'd been *in love* with him? So what? What does it matter? That's what Ivy wants to tell her. *You loved him, is that it? You loved him that way? Well, that's okay. That's nothing. That's lovely. It doesn't matter. Nothing has to matter so much, Clover. Love. Death. Family. None of it.*

Hugging goodbye, they could be strangers submitting to a foreign custom.

It takes hours for the journey (the first train then the second) to enter countryside. Everything is suburbs. The whole country feels like one long town, like she hasn't yet left. But she's on a fast, slaloming train now, making few stops, borne on a feeling that she's moving forward. She's swift. She's light. She's alone.

'Is it free?'

A man puts his leg into the space beside her. For a moment she thinks it's him. The Geologist. Then she doesn't know which 'him' she thought it was. Did she mean Keele? The man, in this braced stance, half in the aisle, half in the seat, launches a hefty duffel bag onto the overhead shelf. It lands like a body. He gets in beside her. She thinks of the Geologist, entering the car with her, leaving the Southern Royal, that first night.

He might be twenty-six or forty-five, this man. She hasn't quite looked right at him. He might be pleasant. He might be terrible. He's a larger than average man. His thigh and knee and elbow encroach on her. Ivy can't blame him for his size. *Stop judging people!* She shouldn't think anything about him. She has no idea about anyone, she realizes now. Any man might be as interesting on the inside as the Geologist is. Any woman, like Clover, might be saying one thing but meaning something else entirely. You should try to like everyone.

They've acknowledged one another to a sufficient extent, she and this man. Now they ably ignore each other. She puts her head back. She closes her eyes, squandering her window seat. She seems to start to sleep. As she dozes, if she really is sleeping, she thinks she's consciously making up her dream, creating it. She keeps coming around to flickering light then sinking back into it.

In the dream, she's sitting with a boulder. It's the size of a large, crouched man. In the dream, she seems to sit with it for hours, this rock, but it never makes a move. The whole dream is very still. Then she's sure she's awake. Then she's sleeping again. And the boulder's an egg. And to it, she puts the bell of a stethoscope, hears its heartbeat. She taps it, strokes it, sings to it. When it hatches, inside is another boulder, smoother, shinier, so sleek it's almost slimy.

When this hatches too, a green shoot rushes up. It quickly thickens, thrusts up, becoming a tree like an oak. Now every limb of the tree strains with nutshells the size of watermelons. Then these burst open, and a whole family of boulders tumble down on her, clonking her shoulders, her arms. They roll around her ankles like a lot of jolly, severed heads…

Waking, she gasps at what's upon her. They're coursing through a landscape, a valley below, high hills above. And a steep, white slope as tall as a skyscraper is leaning right over her. It's about to come down on her. Down like a white wave. No, it's only the sway of the train. But seeing the hill above her, she'd caught a horrific memory rising up inside, and she'd gasped.

'You all right?' says the man beside her.

She looks him in the eyes. Her hand is on top of his. She grabbed it when the train jolted. Now she still grips his hand. Her hand, on his hand, on the armrest.

Ivy! What are you doing? Are you about to sleep with this man, too?!

There was snow on the tops of those hills the train sped through. And the landscape grows snowier, across the border. Then more and more snow. Then snow is falling like it fell the night the Geologist came to stay. In Ivy's city, the snow is really coming down, more, more, really falling, really coming down, by the time she arrives back at her flat.

The door – odd – is open.

The Geologist is standing in the kitchen – Oh, hello – a black coat, a small hill of snow on each shoulder, like epaulets, muddy boots, the tiles muddy from different boots... 'Ivy, the cat...' He'll be somewhere. How was your Christmas? 'No, I saw him. As I came in. Just got here. Looked back. There he was. In the garden. Just now. In the snow. Gone.' But did you leave the door open? As you came in? You know not to leave the door open. What are you telling me? She's saying this as she's turning, stepping back into the garden, still speaking to him. How did you get in? What are you doing here? How did he get out? What's he doing? She's speaking to him even if she isn't near him now, even if he's behind her, as she's going back into the snow, all this snowfall swallowing everything, swallowing her voice, as she's hurrying for the steps, the gate, the lane, calling for Berry, Berry, Berry in a high-strung sing-song, into the darkening, whitening world.

27.

Snow. The mountain man. And my blackness. I call to him. As I enter the garden. As he comes into the kitchen, I enter the garden. One in. One out. We pass. He doesn't see us passing. I stop on my four black legs. And look back. Call to him. *Coming?* Snow coming down. Call again. *Psst! Coming?* He hears it now. My weak little cry. Across the great muffling noise of snow. Sound of snow falling. A sound like a heavy coat pulling on. *Muffle. Scuffle. Shuffle. Shovel.* And my voice. *What are you waiting for?* He hears it. Hears me. He sees me, black in the white garden. A black word on the page of a book. *Hey!* Then I'm gone. I'm

running for the bushes. Into a rustle of leaves. And leaping for the wall. At an angle to the world. Rallying against gravity. Atop. Over. In the lane. I call for him again. I wait. He saw me. I know he saw me. Took the bait. I'm the bait. Wait. Then lead him to the nemesis. Lead him to his doom. The nemesis: somewhere. But where? Just wait. Call for the mountain man. I call for the mountain man. And *she* appears. Her. All of a sudden. All at once. It's her. Her. In the snow. Beautiful as a ghost. Transparent as a ghost. Coming from the road. Pulling red luggage. Coming up the lane in a swirl of white. Like the neighbour cat. Long like the neighbour cat. Legs like the neighbour cat. Bare neck like the neighbour cat. Seductive as the neighbour cat. I'm quiet. Head down, she passes, heads through the gate. Open. Shut. Gone. Whiteness, snow. Walls, snow. Gate, snow. Skittering and dancing, snow. Tunnel of snow. One way: the road. One way: the cherry park. Again garden gate agape.

Her, again. She turns away. Hurries off. She's searching. Seeking me. Calling *Berry Berry Berry*. But I'm not Berry. I'm the promise, the omen, the nemesis. She's calling, but I don't want her. Him. It's him I'm after. And she's gone. Towards the road, streets, neighbourhood. Gone. Again the gate opens, and it's him, so I call. I run. I stop. Look back. Call again. Run. My pawprints are breadcrumbs, disappearing. My voice is breadcrumbs, gone. Snow coming down like ash. A shadow in the snow, I call. I disappear. *This way. Follow me.* Every step a disappearance into a disappearance. Snow swallowing. As I call. And disappear into the cherry park. And call.

And disappear. Into a white glade. White circle. Turn about. Circle about. This way, that way. Pawprints patterning, disappearing. Eye of the storm. Avalanche of blossom. Call for him. *Here, big man! Find me!* I wait for him. For the mountain man. And for the third being, the black-hatted nemesis. Somewhere in the bushes, the black-hatted nemesis, hiding, hidden, waiting. Hiding violence. The black hat. Ready with death. The black hat. Here, where it will happen. An opening in the snowfall, here. Downfall of the mountain man. *Here*. When it will happen. Where it will happen. Where it's about to

but doesn't. He isn't. Hasn't. The mountain man doesn't appear. Hasn't come this way. Calls me. But isn't here. Calls me – *Berry* – but he's further off. Calling, *Berry*. Deep and low. Lower than anything. Lower than snow-sound. *Berry*. Terrifying. *Berry*. Too low, too deep, the voice of the mountain man. Nothing a cat would run to. But I run to it. Running now beside a hoarding. Running into snow, out of snow. Hoarding sliding beside me, into snow, out of snow. As I run, as I call. As I hear him. Smell him. Smell bins-kitchens-people-petrol-trees-rats-cat-cat-dog-cat-fox-him... I slip beneath parked vehicles. I crawl beneath them, slither over oily dry pitches, car by car by car by... Listen for him. Is he here? Hear. Is he near? I hear something. Him? I'm under a car. Under a bumper. Is it him? His growly breath? His heavy panting? I peer out from under, and... a dog! Pulling for me. Pulling at its lead, swinging its boxing-glove face. So, flee. Run. Flee. Terror. Traffic. Sleet. Teeth. A swerving car. Barrage of traffic! Slipshod. Beastly. Churning. Charging. Flee. Fly.

I stop, finally. Stop running and yelling. I stop. No big man. No scent of him. I call for him but I've lost him. Lost. I call for anyone but I'm alone. I'm standing on a long, wide street. Warehouses, apartments, railway arches, walls, kerbs, streetlamps, everything descending, sliding out of sight, sliding into snowfall, into blindness, slipping. And no big man. Nothing. No one. The whole world empty. Windows and pavements pouring away like water. Far-off cars career, spraying grey chowder. But silence here. Nothing. Lost. I've lost. I'm lost. A lost cat. Then: 'Berry?'

Yes, it's me, I'm Berry, here I am, standing in the road. In the whiteness. All walls lost. Just snow. And the road. And the black cat, me. And, 'Berry, there you are,' he says, the big man, coming towards me. 'Come on,' he says and *Come on* I say, waiting in the road. And he is, he's coming for me. He's coming. And up the street now, at the corner, it comes, too. His fate, his destiny, his end, it comes. So, wait. Wait for it. Wait for him, as it comes: the *Good Tidings Fishmonger*'s van. The *Good Tidings*

Fishmonger's van turns the corner, skidding at the corner by the red church. So, just wait. Wait. Be the blackest thing in all this whiteness. Be the perfect omen. As it comes. As he steps into the road.

Read it perfectly, in all this whiteness: *Good Tidings Fishmonger: Something fishy this way comes…* Read its perfect lettering, in all this whiteness, as it hurtles, as it comes… then jump… as he bends, as he grabs… as it comes, the *Good Tidings* fish van, as it comes askew, as the *Good Tidings* van, the *Good Tidings* wheels releasing their scream, as it skids, as it spins… And I seem to catch myself. I seem to come off its flank. Somersault. Cartwheel. Strange interactions, strange intersections: man, van, cat… And there was a roar. There was a boom. A scream, a boom, a roar. And dropping like a horse. There's the scream of the wheels then the boom of the side of the van and his roar and the pile of him in the road. The pile of mountain man in the road. And I'm on my feet, landing on my feet, at the roadside. Gasping. Showing all my teeth. Showing the fleshy insides of my cheeks. Thinking, 'WOW! It's done.' In the road, the big still body. In the road, his big body still. The van stops. The van's growling then silent. The fishmonger opens his door, climbing out, saying, 'What have I done?' Done. It's done, so, go, Berry. Go, get gone, go. Snow coming down in curtains and curtains.

28.

Maybe they needed space, he and she.

'Space?' said Keele. 'You want to call it a day? You want to end it?'

End it? What did Keele mean by that? Why always leap to the most dramatic idea? End it? Ivy really did wonder what he meant by that. End what? Maybe he meant even more than she thought. He really did worry her with talk like that. No, they should get away, she said. They should get some air.

Maybe it was the flat. Her head was feeling claustrophobic, stuffy. She felt like a burrow animal. Maybe everything was really coming from the flat, and not the two of them. Maybe they themselves were actually good, were really fairly good.

Ally and Laine had moved out, not together but diverging, heading in different directions, making their own ways. So, Ivy and Keele really were just the two of them now. Together, they were spreading themselves out in this new space, checking their wingspans.

Wasn't it a good thing? Wasn't it what they'd been waiting for? They really could begin. But begin what? The questions didn't come from inside her but wafted around the dim rooms where she kept passing through them. *So, you really live together now, do you? Is this your life together? Is this the home you have together? What next? Marriage? Promotion? Children?*

'Space?' he said. 'You want to split up?'

No, not space from each other. All she'd meant was they should get out of the flat, take a walk around the block, because the problem was probably the flat and probably not something else. And hadn't he just said, 'I never wanted this flat, your flat, bought and paid for by your dad'? Hadn't he said that? Hadn't he said, 'What am I doing here? I know very well it's not my place and never was. I never said it was. Never needed it or wanted it.' Hadn't he said all that?

What she hadn't said, certainly, was: Get a job! She hadn't said it and she hadn't meant it. If he'd heard that, it wasn't coming from her. What she'd meant was maybe this was an opportunity. Maybe they could really decide something, could see it as a moment to really choose. She'd meant that they were at a crossroads now that Ally and Laine had gone.

'A crossroads? Who talks like that? At a crossroads, are we? Now that Ally and Laine have gone? Now that

Ally and Laine have gone and forked right off? A cross-roads, is it?'

But wasn't it? Wasn't it a crossroads? She was sorry her metaphor wasn't up to scratch. All she'd said was they could think now about what they were doing, where they were going...

'I know all that,' he said. 'I know the answers to that. What I'm doing is being with you. Where I am is with you. Where I'm going is wherever, but always with you. I'm not here for the flat or the city or a career but for you.'

We can't live on poetry, Iain. We can't eat poetry.

'These poems, Ivy. All these poems. They're for you.'

Are you sure? I don't recognize myself at all. Aren't they really about you?

'How can that be true? It's all about you. Always. It's you I'm trying to see.'

But you get in the way. It's me being looked at but you doing the looking. It's not always easy, being looked at so closely...

'Maybe you're right. Maybe you're right and we should get some space. You're right. Let's take a walk. Get some air, maybe,' and somehow her plan for a neighbourhood stroll had been turned into something else. A mountain. Open sky. A drive away from the city.

*

In the car, they didn't argue. They didn't speak. Wordlessly, she slid in an old CD he liked, as if posting him a letter. It was a band from here, where neither of them was from. It was a small, shiny slice of the reason they'd ended up here. The series of sparkly, talky little songs fluttered up around their heads, around the headrests and the rear-view mirror, like dust motes in the sunlight. Blue shadows on the road. Golden hills. A bright hillside holding close to its chest a dense field of pines. And the pines were the shape of a dark green fish leaping. It was summer about to be autumn.

At the car park, she wanted to walk to the water. But he was heading for the mountain. 'Not a mountain, Ivy,' he said. 'A hill.' She looked. She took it in, the lower slopes, the pine wood rising like a green wave. They weren't dressed for the climb. Their trainers weren't up to it.

'Only a hill,' he said again. 'You wanted space. Room to breathe. Didn't you? Well, this is it.' That hadn't been her meaning of 'space', of course, but they were here now. Here they were. She said he was right, and he said, 'No, it's you who's right. That's what I'm saying.'

They followed the waymarkers and were soon walking a gentle, curving rise, trees spreading out on either side. The hill seemed to build itself higher and higher before them, the ground mounting and mounting, mound by mound. She said out loud that things were really going to escalate up ahead. Then she regretted what sounded like a criticism. She said she meant it was going up and up, hill by hill.

'Like a lolloping puppy,' said Keele, which she didn't really quite get. But it was pretty. A pretty picture. So, maybe he was right and they were happy, and maybe it was the right route, the right choice to come out here, and they were sticking together.

They entered the pines. As they went, Keele collected bits and pieces of this and that – a leaf, bark, moss… Holding a snail shell up to his eye, he said, 'What's in here? Any mysteries? It might have a poem inside it.' They hadn't picked up their argument again.

A winding ascent, beneath the trees. Roots elbowed from the ground: steps they took. It was pleasant. The shade quenched them. The ground was soft and crumbly like bread. They cleared a stile and came out under the sun again. After the pines: spine of the hill. Up there. Distant little walkers. Making their way against the glorious sky. But she and Keele weren't there yet. A staircase of stones began, a harder climb, hugging the side of the slope.

Below them, the green hillside folded over in a deep crease, and in there an unseen stream ran away. A gloomy glitter. She heard it running, back into the woods, and towards the car park. Then her eye was drawn out into the wide, low landscape to the south, the fields lying like a sheeny lake. Further off, she saw the beginnings of the towns at the peripheries of the city they'd left. Somewhere amongst all that, lying low in the cityscape, was the flat.

The top of the hill looked more distant now. You kept thinking you'd got nearer then at the next crest or turn it moved away again. The incline had eased. A high, grassy valley – a sort of plateau – had opened up. They continued at an amble, sometimes scrambling over broad, stone ledges through which water trickled. The valley was a lawn. From somewhere, Keele produced an apple-shaped rock and placed it on top of a cairn.

Was that allowed? How long had the cairn stood there? Weeks or centuries? What did a cairn mean? Could absolutely anyone add to the pile, no matter how little of a way they'd come? And why couldn't she stop questioning him?

'If you think it's one too many,' he said, 'let's restore the balance.' Then, from halfway down the cone of stones, he pulled out a rock of similar size, but slim, jagged. For a moment, it seemed like the cairn might fall, tumble apart like a tower of oranges in the supermarket. There was a shifting and sliding of surrounding stones. But it resettled itself. Keele opened his jacket and slipped the shard into his inside pocket. He patted his chest. 'Close to my heart. Okay, this way.'

But it wasn't that way. The direction he took off in, that wasn't the way. It wasn't the waymarked trail to the summit, and had they even agreed to go the whole distance?

'Did we agree to anything?' he said. 'Do we have to know exactly where we're headed? Why always stick to the path, Ivy?'

Here we go again, she said. We're onto this again, are we? What difference does it make? Why do you need *not* to take the path? What difference does it make to you, Iain, whether we take the rambler's route or a sheep track, if this whole country's so domestic to you? You don't want to be here. That's what we're getting at. Go off if you want to, but I know what you'll find. You'll find you don't want to be anywhere. I hope you find somewhere. I really do.

He was irritated now. 'Where's this coming from? Did I say any of that? Thanks for the diagnosis, Doctor Dover!' So, now it was the 'doctor' line of argument, again, the 'doctor's-daughter-doctor' line of argument, the argument about how Ivy didn't know who she was or what she was or what she really wanted, because she'd simply donned the hat marked 'doctor' as a teenager, and had never taken it off again, because she'd simply followed in her father's footsteps, those polished, black, ringing footsteps... Or maybe she knew too well what she wanted, had always known too well, had never thought for herself. Was that it? There were various ways to spin it, to swing for her. This time, he was saying that she didn't know herself at all, that she'd lost herself in 'doctoring', that she understood bones and lungs and brains and even hearts but nothing about souls.

'You're so much in your world,' he said, 'that you can't see the wood for the trees.'

She was tired. Was it so wrong to know yourself? If, turning the corners of wards, with a series of duties before her, she knew with certainty where she was, and what she was, was that so wrong? Wasn't it better than this? So often, around Keele, she felt uncertain. She felt like an unstable cairn of shaky stones, stone after stone removed by Keele's hand.

If you're going, go. If we're breaking up, get on with it. Had she just said that? Or did she only think it? Difficult in the heat of the argument to remember. Hold on. Work back. Who said what? Was it said yet? Was she about to say it? Was it already over or about to be over? She thought of worn-out, doctorly lines.

Like ripping off a plaster.

This will sting a little.

No cure for a broken heart.

She turned away. She turned towards the way back. I'm going this way, she said. She said she'd see him at home.

'Home?' he said. 'Home, is it? At home there, are you? You could have fooled me.' He paused. They looked at each other. He said, 'Okay, see you. Just, see you.' And she said, See you, too. Then he left the path and set off awkwardly across scrubby, uneven terrain, towards the scraggy, unscalable face of the peak.

She stood there. She watched him, without being too obvious about it. He never looked back, being obvious about it. He grew smaller and smaller, quickly. The size of a child, then a cat, then a bird. She thought of sitting on the grass. She thought of continuing to the top alone, following the path. She might meet him up there. She might beat him to it. How would that play out? How would that go down? Maybe they'd laugh.

A little way further on, at the crest of this valley, just a little way into the next rise, it was about to become spectacular, she knew. She could continue only that far, to where it opened up. It was about to open up: the slopes, the water, the forested shores; and the fecund, muffin-like islands on the water; and the breezy white flecks of a distant sailing school; and that expansive, silver surface of the water seeming to speak its depths...

Instead, she went down the hill – a quick, skippy descent – heading for their car (her car), the city, the flat.

Free now to saunter and stumble as she pleased, she noticed her surroundings. She discovered a tangle of blackberries growing gorgeous and oozy. She picked them carelessly, not minding the pricks to her thumbs. She re-entered the wood.

At one moment, deep in the dark of the pine forest, turning back, she thought she caught a final glimpse of him, out there, up there, tiny and dazzlingly lit, slipping and putting out a hand against the wall of the hill. The sharp slope confused his body. At an angle to the world. Rallying against gravity.

It would be the last time she saw him, if that was him. It would be the last time, because this was them ending it, wasn't it? Those years were over, and whether it had been good or bad the job now was to move on. The job was to go through your everyday tasks as you moved towards moving on. It felt like grief. It felt childish to say so.

But it would, wouldn't it, be the last time she saw him? Next time, he wouldn't be him. She wouldn't be her. It would be the last time she was what she was to him, the last time he was what he was to her; the last time he was him.

29.

By the wall of the red sandstone church... against a long, pebble-dash shed... in the dead flowerbed, with a camping chair and broken bottles lying about, and stalks of lifeless buddleia like a clump of walking sticks... Berry rests... Berry, resting... Berry's pulse and panic subsiding, and snow falling steadily, snow falling lightly now... and Berry... Admit it, Berry, you felt high, seeing the van knock him down. Thrilling, seeing your death up close. You come alive, don't you, in those dangers. Poor cat, you come alive when you die, don't you, thinking, 'Now this is living!' Sky. Ground. Air. Trees. Everything comes alive, everything sings... Poor cat. It's okay. Cat, I'm here. I'm here. To stroke your fur. To come out of myself. To stroke your back, rub between your ears, as you calm down. To say, 'There, there, cat,' as your heartbeat slows, as our heartbeat slows... maybe too slow now, the cold setting in on us, where we lie, Berry. Berry and me. Body and soul. The omen-cat and the promise fulfilled. We're love. We do love her. It's love... All we do. All we've done... Trying to show her. Trying to know her. Couldn't get close enough. Couldn't feel right enough. Never enough... If I could say sorry... Sorry for everything... No good at being a cat. No good at anything. No good at being. If I could have been good to her, fair to her, kind to her... If I could have loved her like she deserved... But that would have meant being selfless, would have meant coming out of myself... Never managed it, not even now. Can't let her go. Even now, I can't seem to leave... But it's possible... Soul loosening. Heart so slow now... Possible to think more clearly. Like I'm growing clearer. And rising like air... and Berry growing colder, more still. Berry lying below me. Looking far-off. Looking small, black, still. Looking like a black hat, left out in the snow... as I'm lifting, as I'm lifting into branches of the cherry trees, dying... Dead, and she doesn't know I'm dying. Dead, and I don't know it. Dead, and floating. In love, and floating... Ivy, it wasn't enough. I'm sorry. Ivy, it isn't enough but I'm sorry... Wanting you, beseeching you, having you, keeping you... The most selfish thing I ever did on Earth, not letting you go... I wasn't true. I was never true. I was the spectre of bad love. Living or dead, I was never true... And cold and black, Berry, you're far below me now, the string about to snap, a balloon bobbing in these branches... *Berry*. Far away. *Berry*. Your name they're calling, not mine, Berry. You he's looking for, not me. *Berry. There you are, Berry.* You he's found, not me. He's found you, the mountain man, the big man, alive and limping... and crouching over you now, opening his large coat... and standing... and I see you, the cat, the black thing, soggy and slack, as he takes you, takes you into himself... hurrying off, thumping off for the flat... the flat there... the garden wall, kitchen window... as I'm drifting, like I'm dreaming, letting go, letting go of you, letting go of her, of me, letting go of... I'm sorry, Ivy... I'm sorry... I should have left you the hell alone...

30.

Berry's dead and gone, she knows it. Though she stays out looking, she's already formulating her own party line. *A fox got him,* she might say. Or: *Eaten by a fox,* adding that bit of brutality. More decisive. More dead. *Dead.* A good word. Onomatopoeic. Falling with a thud, like wood.

He was a good cat, she's ready to say. But to whom? To Clover? She doesn't know if she and Clover are speaking. But if she isn't about to say this to Clover then who to? The neighbours? Who would need to know? The world won't need to be informed. There'll be no state funeral.

He was a good cat. The past tense is in place. That 'cat' and that 'good', they speak for themselves. Make of it what you will, depending on your feelings for cats, depending on your history with cats. Whether it matters or not, it doesn't matter. It was a dead, good cat. A good, dead cat. That's it. It's sad.

She keeps waiting for the moment she'll turn back, as she spirals out from her home, taking wider and wider digressions into the snowfall, street upon street. People run doubled over. Everyone's clothes look wet and black. Someone's cursing. Somebody thinks it's hilarious. Headlights whisk snowflakes all over the place, like whites in a washing machine. You can't see further than half a block. The streets and parks and workplaces and schools and trainlines and expressways, the river, the university... it's all eaten up. Nothing exists but this neighbourhood.

She can't see anything, so what's the point? She can't see anything and the cat's dead, so what's the point? Sometimes she tries to check her phone, pressing at the sleety screen with her gloved hand. She takes the glove off and tries to dry the device on her wet coat, dib-dabbing with stiffening fingers.

Anything?

But never a message from the Geologist or anyone, until a caption slides up saying: 'Sorry. Hands full of cat. I have him. Come home.'

In the flat, all the lights and lamps are on, the heating heightened. It's like a real home. Hardly feels like her home at all. Not the one she thought she lived in. This place is more complete, more contained, all those lights glowing, and the furniture gathered around the lights.

The sofa, the armchair, a table, they cast a family of warm shadows. Berry and the Geologist sit together. She's come into a room to find them, man and cat, sitting together.

It's the Geologist's doing, the light and warmth. She'd got used to being cold, feeling it in her wrists, the back of her neck, between her shoulders. But he, the Geologist, he wants the home warmed to the bone. She's happy to. He's someone to warm it for. She thinks of Tiger, her nephew. Someone to make a Christmas for. The Geologist, he's like a boy you have.

The spare room is mended too now. It's days later. Days pass. It's mended. Repainted, too. The spare room walls. A new carpet, days later. It's here they dine together, on the carpet tonight. She's thinking she might move in here, or thinking of other ways to rearrange the flat. Rooms rearranged. Rooms in all different places. They feel new (she thinks), sitting on the carpet with their legs stretched out, leaning back against the wall. The way they're sitting, it's where her bed used to be, when Keele lived with her, when Keele was alive.

At their feet, Berry's quiet as a cushion while they eat. In their hands, they cup hot bowls: rice, egg, pickle, spice. The food steams muggily. They lower their faces. They're people from the past and it's the insides of a creature they've caught and killed in a snowy wilderness, and they're eating it right there and then, right at the moment of killing, out in the snow…

When I first moved up here, she says, someone told me, *We have two seasons – winter, and everything else. Each lasts half the year. Half winter, half everything else.* Then they said, *We're really in it now, aren't we? The winter. How's yours going?* I liked that. I liked that you could meet a stranger and ask if they were getting on all right, or say there was light at the end of the tunnel, and they knew what you meant. It's like we're all in this together. It's grim but it's ours. It made me feel like I belonged…

In hot countries, she goes on. In hot countries, it seems like they meet in the street, in the squares, drinking and meeting outside. Maybe close friends never even see inside each other's homes. But, here, we always meet indoors, light fires, put lights on, get under the blankets, invent hot cocktails. It must make us different. You must make friends differently, keep friends differently, eat and drink differently, make love differently, fall in love differently, in a cold country.

'I couldn't be somewhere hot,' he says, and she wonders again where he comes from, where he fits. What's his natural habitat? 'You go where the work is, as a geologist,' he says, 'but I couldn't be somewhere hot. Truth is,' he continues, 'there are two types of work a geologist can do. Search for water or search for oil. Oil or water, that's your job, whether you like it or not. But you don't. What you like is rocks, if you're a geologist.'

Oil? Well, we do need it, I suppose.

'You'd think searching for water was better,' he answers. 'But I don't see much difference. Either way, you're sucking the planet dry. Every last drop of carbon or H_2O we can squeeze out of the ground. All last-ditch stuff. Not what folk who love millennia would enjoy. Not what you want your life's work to be, not if you've loved this planet since you were a boy...'

Listening, she thinks again how much truth and decency there is to him and – Just say it! – how much allure, how much handsome, physical allure... and how much intelligence and wit and care, and delicious, hunky reticence... a passion so epic and slow that you don't even see it. He's gorgeous. She's happy.

She's slowing right down. Being with him is like being with a mountain, so close you can't conceive of it for what it is, so far-off you can't comprehend it either. No sense of scale. So, she's slowing right down. She hasn't seen him. She hasn't understood him. But now she can. She can see him better and better. And now that she knows how wonderful he is, she knows she's let him down. It's time she let him go.

'So, the university job was only ever short-term,' he's saying. 'That's the point I'm trying to make. A few months. The way jobs go. Always would be short. Was always going to be. Never would've metamorphosized into anything. Never would be something more set in stone. Couldn't help hoping. Not like I don't want roots.

A life. Not like I want to go town to town "gathering no moss" forever. But not on the cards. You go where the jobs are. And the jobs are far-flung. Few and far between.

'I'm sorry, is what I'm saying,' he says. 'Feel like I've been stringing you along. I was due to leave when we were just getting to know each other. When it came around to pay more rent at One-Two, it was already time to move on. But you and me were getting on so well... Well, I thought I could stay a bit longer. I moved out of the room at One-Two and sort of... hung around. Always knew it wasn't going anywhere. But I liked you. Got the idea you liked me, too...

'Only, now the new job's been in touch. They'll need me sooner. Flight's booked. Sorry. Don't know why I'm saying sorry. Never going to stay, was I? You weren't thinking that. I'm not what you had in mind. I know that. Not in the long run. Can't argue with you. We don't make sense. I know how I seem. I know I'm difficult. My brother's the same. Two chips off the same old block. Not good guys. Not a good family. I try but I'm nothing special. Not like you.'

As he talks, the room seems to grow warmer, seems to warmly glow. The outside darkens. It's safe in here. It's wet and dark outside. She thinks she can hear the end of winter. She thinks she can hear the ice melting and running away. Water seeps into the lawn and into the ground below the flat, running under the floorboards and down towards the river.

'… taking some getting used to,' he's saying. 'New country. New folks with new ways. Rocky road ahead. Mountainous country. Like here but more than here. Somewhere more mountainous than here. Somewhere more northern than here. New language to learn but, you know, not so different. A bairn over there is a *barn*. I'm in your hoose here, Ivy, and when I'm there it'll be my *hus*. For me, you know, a stone is a *stain*. Don't use these words with you, not much. Talk to you so you can hear me. Meet you where you are. But I grew up a bairn throwing stains in the burn. And when I'm there a stone'll be a stein. A stone is a stain is a stein…'

As she listens to him, she doesn't know what to do with her face. Unquestionably, she agrees. He will leave. This will end. This has always been ending. Isn't it what she was always thinking?

She puts down her bowl. She lays her head on his shoulder. He's still talking. It's warm in the room. It's cold in the world.

'Look, I'm in love with you, as it happens,' he says. 'But that's probably not enough. Probably wouldn't be enough even if you loved me, too, which you don't. You don't, and I'm not asking you to. You like me, and that's all I want. But you've got a life here. Friends. Career. A home. A cat! This place here, you're really building a home. I don't have anything like that. Never did. Never expected you to come with me. Don't get me wrong. Not asking you to. I leave in a few days. I can go sooner if you like. Somewhere more mountainous. Somewhere colder and darker than here, if you can believe it.'

31.

When no call or message came from Keele, she took it as confirmation it was over. It was closed. She couldn't have called him to make sure, because that would have opened it up again. That would have opened again the possibility of it continuing at least a little longer, a little way further. It would have never quite finally ended. Silence was the only workable answer.

Hours later, with still no sign of him, she lay down in their room. She'd have to stop saying *our bed*. She got up and changed the sheets. Was there malice in that? Was there aggression in making the bed? What if he came back? Where else would he sleep tonight? Did he even know how to book a hotel room? She felt good, that was the truth of it. She fell asleep feeling the calmness and clarity of knowing a choice had been made.

And when she woke, her thoughts were as crisp and white as hospital cotton. She was light. She was reaching out. Her fingers were still purple with blackberry juice. It was her phone that had woken her because it was still ringing.

The voice said its name and something official. The voice was somehow official. But she couldn't keep hold of whoever it was as she tried to wake up, as she tried to keep up with what they were saying now. She'd closed her eyes again. She lay on her back with a forearm covering her eyes. It was a bright morning outside. She tried again to listen. A question was being asked.

Did she know a man named Iain Keele?

Yes, Iain lives here with me, she said. She felt unsure, speaking so suddenly after sleep. Was her larynx ready? Would the words come out right? He lives with me. *Iain's my boyfriend.* But why would she say that? He wasn't. Not anymore. So, why say that?

Then when she said next, Is he all right? why say that, too? Why wouldn't he be?

At the Southern Royal, the people there, if they didn't know her well, the people there, everyone, they knew her somewhat. In fact, she was meant to be working that day but at another of the infirmaries, in another compass point of the city.

A nurse, recognizing Ivy, called her out on it.

'Wrong hospital, Doctor Dover! Wrong invalids!'

Then the nurse stopped and looked at her again. Ivy

wasn't dressed for the job. She hadn't showered. She was dressed shambolically. Diabolically. Jeans pulled on over pyjamas. No make-up. A large coat over a T-shirt that read *Joie de Vivre*. Doctors don't necessarily arrive 'prepped for surgery' but the nurse noted it.

'Didn't recognize you out of uniform!'

Ivy must have looked a state. She felt caught out. She must have looked – God forbid! – like a patient, without all the armour to keep herself the right side of the line. That was it. The nurse was looking at her like she was a patient or the loved-one of a patient. The nurse looked at her with kindness. This was the day it began, her hatred for nurses.

'Actually, you look really quite lovely,' said the nurse. 'You should wear your hair down more often. And your skin looks lovely. That's what a good night's sleep will do for you, no doubt. But my husband, he's a snorer, he's a sprawler, he's a canoodler…'

Nice to see you, said Ivy, turning away. Must get going. Just popped in. Just some documents… This and that to sign off, you know how it is. I'm not really here.

No, she wouldn't be a patient. She wouldn't be pitied. She was a colleague. She found the toilets. She washed her face. She built herself back up. She'd be a colleague. A professional. Whatever was coming, you could be a professional about it. There were always proper procedures, for whatever situation you found yourself in.

Meeting with the doctor, yes, it was another person she partly knew, but she kept her control. They were colleagues. Ivy took the lead. She set the tone, used the words. *Cranial. Cerebral. Focal. Diffuse. Induced.* When Ivy said the word *trauma* she was using terminology, nothing more, only terminology. As she listened and the doctor spoke, an understanding was maintained between them. It could be presented more as it was, taking away a little of the pretence. There wasn't any pretence that there was anything at all to tell her.

'You'll know how unpredictable these cases can be,' the doctor said. 'You'll know, also, it doesn't look good. You'll know there's hope, but you'll also know that you can't prescribe hope, if you're one of us.'

One of us. She clung to the idea. If she could see this as a doctor would see it... if she could hold on to that... if she could move through it as a doctor... Compassionate. Comprehending. Distant.

'Would you like to see him?'

She didn't spend long alone with him. Who knew what he could hear, or if he could hear, or if he could think, or what he thought of her? It felt like meeting someone you knew very well but out of context – your sister out with her friends; your drama-buff flatmate on the stage in costume... You knew them and you didn't know them.

Your poor head, she said, touching the bandaging gingerly. Were his ideas whirring, even now? A fracture behind the left ear, they said. Not much to see. A small, dark mark. But an intense impact must have happened, likely a collision with a rock when he fell. A series of falls, really. Over some distance. A number of metres. Cartwheeling. Somersaulting.

Cause of Death: loss of balance. He'd simply slipped. His body in the heather had been discovered by chance, through the binoculars of a dawn birdwatcher. Keele's bright trainers, luckily, had caught the eye (but inappropriate footwear for the loose scree of those slopes). What had the twitcher thought, at first, spotting those luminous trainers poking out from the purple heather? *Fancy that! A pair of feral parakeets, this far north?*

'Remarkably unscathed,' said the doctor. (Ivy, of course, was not 'the doctor'). 'Remarkably unscathed, except for the critical head injury.' You might have baulked at this bedside manner if you weren't also in the same line of work. Ivy knew how impossible words were. Words were Keele's talent, not hers. Besides, she wanted all this. Poor people skills. Medical jargon. Anything but sympathy.

'There's some indication, in fact, the police will have told you, that the collapse wasn't instantaneous, that he got himself up again, after the accident itself.'

What does that mean? No, no one had told her anything. But now this image comes like another possible reality, like a chance of a change of fate, Keele falling but standing up again.

The doctor continued. 'As I've explained, there are no broken bones, except for the head. Not even any cuts or bruises. So, he might have felt good. When he got up again. Elated, even. He stood back up, it seems, and walked away. *From the scene*, so to speak. Walked away as if everything was fine and, miraculously, he'd survived without a scratch. He must have been counting his blessings and patting himself all over. You can imagine…

'But then, as you can see, that suddenly stopped.'

32.

To all the Geologist said (including about his loving her), there were ways she could have responded. She could have said the same, or something similar. She could have given a name, then and there, to what it was like for her, being with him, this man, this feeling not felt before, this feeling of safe harbour and snug hunger, this feeling of being with him, this feeling of really liking somebody, of simply liking somebody so much...

But she's been loved before and she didn't love enough, and this time, too, she isn't loving well. The best she can do for anyone is keep her heart to herself. He's right, it wouldn't have made sense. And she does have this flat and the job. And they've served her well. They've been sufficient stand-ins. Maybe it's not a lot to overthrow but there are, if not friends, well, faces, names, familiarities...

But why don't you stay? she said. Just until your move. If you'd like to.

A week later he'll be gone.

In the week leading up to it, they continue just as before, just *being*. Just as before, they live together like it will end at any moment, and like they've always lived like this. In fact, so much does it feel like it did already, living like this, knowing it will end, that she begins to wonder if maybe it won't end, if it will just go on eternally and swimmingly like this, always, forevermore. Is it really final, that day approaching?

They continue to talk, before the end, each showing themselves a bit more, bit by bit, drip by drip. Maybe they say more now, knowing it really will end, really might end. She tells him Keele's name, Iain Keele's whole name, who he was, how he died, what he was like. It's easy. It's suddenly a very long time ago.

At work, she thinks of him, there in her home, the cat and him. Do they go on existing, in that box, when she's not there? The Geologist. The cat.

At the Southern Royal, a nurse: 'Someone was looking for you, Doctor Dover. A man.'

Odd of the nurse to say it like that. *Someone looking. A man. For you.* Aren't people looking for people all the time in hospitals? *Paging Doctor Dover… Doctor Dover to Paediatrics…* But the way she says it, it makes you wonder 'who?' and 'for what?' Ivy remembers waking to a phone call one morning. *Do you know an Iain Keele?*

220

Yes, my boyfriend. Boyfriend. Someone. Man. Looking. Ordinary words, coming out wrong.

'Yes, looking for you,' says the nurse. 'Didn't say your name, but it must have been you he meant. The way he described you. It was obvious. I knew immediately. "It must be Doctor Dover," I said. "That's it. That's her. It must be her. That's Doctor Dover to the letter."'

These nurses! Always meaning something. Or Ivy's sensitive. Yes, that's it. She's overly sensitive. That's it. That's her. It must be her.

But you know this nurse means something by saying 'a *man*', something about Ivy's relationship to men. Just recently, at the Christmas party, she'd been caught hold of by a nurse, lubricated, liquid, fluid in her party gown, who told her, 'You know, we're all women. We're women when we want to be, Doctor Dover. But you, on the other hand, are firstly and lastly and always, no matter what, a doctor. If I cut you, you'd say *doctor* all the way down. You'd bleed *doctor*...'

'I knew he meant you,' this nurse says now. What does she mean by that? What was the description the man gave her? A serious woman? A thin woman? Tall? Pallid? Sour? You know the nurse means more than she says. But what does it matter? Smile. Play along.

Ooo, a man? For me!

'Odd bloke,' says the nurse. 'Something off. Odd. Off. Can't put my finger on it, but you figure it out, don't you?

You spot it. Sorts we get around here. I've been around the block. Blokes like that. A good woman knows a bad 'un when she sees one. A good woman knows a man who's up to something... Wore a hat...'

Every nurse is a private eye. They all blur into one. Always seeming to know something. Or does this woman just exist on intuition, instinct, impulse, like a cat, reading the signs, picking up on signals, catching it all, letting it all go, easy-breezy? A man with a hat.

No, says Ivy, no idea. No, she wouldn't know what that would be about. No idea, she says, though she does have an idea now. She has more than an idea. She's worked it out. She's solved the puzzle.

Yes, she knows about him. Knows who he is. Another of those strange nights at the Southern Royal. Another of those strangers. Plainly clothed. Wore a hat. A hallucination haunting the wards, seeking someone *worse-for-wear*, someone *been-in-the-wars*. She knows, though no one has said anything. Not something she has words for. But she knows...

'Anyway, don't worry,' says the nurse. 'I saw him off. He won't be back round here again. Not this hospital. He'll try his luck elsewhere. We're rid of him. So, don't worry, Doctor Dover. Don't look so worried. Let your guard down once in a while!'

33.

The day before the Geologist leaves, they drive out to the hill Keele fell from. Some snow remains on the mountain-tops and in the deep, shadowy scars of the mountainsides, but not on the hill. In the sky there are piles of grey and white clouds, ruptures of blue. They take a squelchy walk right up to the summit. It's less than an hour to get up there. Nobody falls and kills themselves.

On the climb, a surprising number of small brown birds crop up.

Then: 'Buzzard,' the Geologist says.

She doesn't spot it, but answers, Oh, yes. I'd never have seen that without you here.

They climb.

'This hill,' he says, 'it's on a fault line. Did you know?' He might mean only her: did *she* know? Or maybe he means she and Keele. *Did he know, when he fell, he was falling from the crest of a vast tectonic fracture?*

'Great traumas, Earth goes through,' he says. 'But most folk can't see it. Most folk don't know how to look. Down here. Under our feet. Upheavals. Might not seem it. This little hill. But this is the division. Here. Where the mountains start. To the north, it's mountains. Runs right across the country. Slant. This fault. This fault line. Right here. We're not far out of the city. But this is the boundary. Two different terrains. To the north: mountains. To the south: flat. Two different worlds. High and low. We're straddling it here.'

He takes a wide stance, legs spread across the ridge. And she grins. She's turned on. Even all those clouds arouse her. The hill, too. Everything is muscular.

'It's where I'm from,' he says, gesturing. 'That way. North. Thought I'd never leave. The mountains. Thought I'd never get out from under it. The mountains. But can't change where you're from. Can't change what you're from.'

He rubs at the scar on his forehead. It's healed. A few sandy crumbs of scab brush away, some miniscule pinpricks of blood, maybe. It's healed but maybe it will always show a scar – a fine, white fissure on his grand and rocky brow.

'I want to tell you things,' he says. 'To talk to you. Tell you about me. You don't mind? I want to. Should. About me. About my brother. The old man. But I'm a big boy. I weather it. Weather comes. Weather goes. It's like blaming the weather. Not the weather's fault. Fault of no one. A different life up there. Different landscape. Thought I'd never get out. Not sure I ever have. Change countries but you're still where you're from.'

Then he's gone.

Travelling with him to the airport feels entirely too wifely. So, they say goodbye at the front door. It's short-lived, all of a sudden. She hugs him. He turns away. Then he turns back and kisses her, holding her head in his bear-sized hands, slurping her up like a whelk from the shell. She loves it. The feeling her head is a thing. The feeling she's weightless. She takes a gasp of air, like you do after a good, deep drink of water. Then he really is gone.

It's Ivy again. It's Ivy and the cat. She goes around switching off lamps. She checks the hour hand on all the clocks. Why? The time zone won't have changed. Not for her, but the Geologist will need to put his watch forward now. In the front room, the cat is under the armchair. The cat is halfway under the armchair, turned a quarter towards her. It looks like a cat. Only a cat. It looks blank.

Maybe it's still in shock. Maybe it's still recovering from the near-death experience. The snow. The car accident. Who knows what happened to it out there? Who knows how nearly it really died? She never knew where it came from either, never knew what it had been through, years ago, before it arrived at her door.

I've been neglecting you, haven't I.

Or maybe it isn't shock but absolute calm. Maybe the cat is calm. Maybe they're back to normal, or maybe they're irrevocably changed. *I've been neglecting you.* It isn't an apology. I've been neglecting you, and before that fawning, doting, smothering. Which is worse?

She used to treat her cat like a little husband. She feels sad and silly, remembering how she used to think about that pet. The first cat was her grandmother. The second was her husband. She watches Berry now. Its slit eyes take her in.

Sitting here, she looks ahead. She runs through her schedules, identifies every empty space, ascribes each gap a new and necessary process, builds a busy week. She gets up, sorts the flat, sits, gets up, sits, and whenever she sits again the cat acknowledges her. Isn't that why you own a cat? Isn't that proof they both exist?

34.

When Keele's mother (Lee) got to the hospital, it might have begun a deceit lasting the whole coma or – who knows? – a lifetime. To save complications, Ivy might have said they were still together. But other complications would have resulted. And, looking at Iain in the bed, it was somehow so obvious, so true, that he wasn't hers, that she wasn't his.

So, outside his room, she told Lee: We'd broken up, I think. But it wasn't a nasty break up, not very nasty. He was okay. He wasn't *not in his right mind* or anything like that. He was in his right mind. He was being just like himself. He was off doing what he does. You know what he's like. Is it best if I don't visit him?

'No, come as much as you need,' said Lee.

But what about Lee? Did Lee *need* Ivy to come? The medical insights were valued, that was clear. Lee made that clear.

'What I can't understand is if they're saying he'll live or, or, or…' Lee said. 'These doctors, what do you think? Do they have any idea? They can't seem to say anything. Not anything I can understand. If they could tell us what's going on with Iain's head… Do they know? It reminds me of parents' evenings at school when he was a little boy. Talking to these doctors, it's like talking to his teachers. You always wondered if they really knew your child. It's like listening to riddles. Iain likes all that. Riddles. Tricksy language. Just give it to me straight. That's what I want. Just tell me he'll be okay. Just give it to me straight. Unless it's bad news…'

In the end, it would be Lee who was there, not Ivy. It would be Lee who would call Ivy, weeping, gulping, 'My boy. Our Iain.'

But before that moment, Ivy would have to tell him goodbye. In her head, she went over and over this goodbye. She had said it once already – *goodbye* – halfway up that hill. This was only a goodbye like that again. It didn't mean more. She knew they weren't together, and so did he, a part of him. It was over. It wasn't right. She couldn't keep returning.

She'd accepted (without melodrama or martyrdom, she assured herself) the weight, upon herself, of his terrible accident. Not her fault, but there was guilt for her to take and she took it, here and now. As a doctor (she clung to that again), it wasn't her first accidental death. They were all accidents really, she sometimes thought, all those hospital deaths, a whole universe of accidents, the things you saw at work, the endpoints of violence, stupidity, missteps, unfairness, randomness… Why not call them all 'terrible accidents' and grieve for everyone?

What she thought about most, in the days of the coma, was the idea of Keele getting up from his fall. She couldn't shake it. Her mind, wandering, went to it. Or she dreamt it. She saw him lying there, moments after coming to a stop. She saw him blinking, on his back. It was a cool, blue sky that day. You could think it was hot one minute, cold the next. His eyes would have been full of sky and hill. His heart would have been pounding. She thought of him laid out under that sky, smiling at the sky. She thought of him as a vast expanse of water, reflecting the sky.

He got up. She saw him get up, pretty nimbly, puffing, laughing, feeling the life all over his living body, in his chest and his hands and his legs. That laughter was important. The movement and bounce in his limbs. He would have been happy. He was inside that moment. She'd seen him like that, now and again. Nine hundred and ninety-nine thousand, nine hundred and ninety-nine times out of a million he was in his head. But he loved to be in the moment, laughing, talking, chasing a train. She loved him, in those rare moments.

She loved the thought of him standing again. She'd never loved anything so much as the image of him standing and laughing after his fall. She didn't love him, not romantically, but she loved that image more than anything. She didn't love him. But she imagined him waking suddenly from this coma, just like that, standing, puffing, laughing, patting himself all over. A changed man. She loved him.

She wished the doctor hadn't told her about him standing again. The most painful and beautiful thing she could ever imagine, Keele standing again. Her soul lurched to think of it, like she was in a rowboat with Keele, and he was on his feet, legs braced, making a great joke of rocking them about.

At some point, she saw him for the last time. He was in his coma. He was dead to the world. Alone with him, she recited aloud and from memory, the entirety of 'If I Was Your Cat'. She told him that she loved his poem and was thankful for it. She told him she loved him. She felt like a mother to him, the way she spoke. He was a young man. Not really a child. But a child.

If I was your cat, I'd kill you a velvet mouse.
If I was your cat, I'd kill you a jewelled bird.
I'd bring you larger cats, cast in gold.

I'd bring a dead dog. Bigger things:
livestock, zoo animals, predators native to our wilds,
a horse, a man, a child.

If I was your cat, I'd be your watchdog, all trespass
unforgiven. I'd be the jungle beast at your door.
Guest or host or ghost, I'd find a way in.

Have me in your lap. Feel my purring inside.
Forget that I'm a cat at all, your eyes
rolled back. Caress me like I'm a man's arm.

I won't be anything. I'll be less
and less. I'll be your son,
your daughter. I'll be no one.

I'll be water, taking the shape of my vessel,
filling every corner of your house,
pouring myself out into you.

A prayer.

That same evening, finally, she needed to tell him that she wouldn't come again. He'd lain, Iain, in the bed and made no reaction as she spoke. He was underwater. He was the calmest he'd ever been, connected to his IV. Ivy had never been 'a crier' and her training had only perfected the talent. But the words played out badly. This part wasn't the other doctor's skill. It had never been Ivy's skill either. It was for the best that no one heard her.

They were high up in the Southern Royal. She'd been working in a different hospital of the city. She was exhausted. She kept turning away to the window. The sky was violet and granite. The summer was over. The low, distant hills to the north had just about faded away. His hill was somewhere among them, the one he'd fallen from. Lights were coming on all over the hospital complex, on the paths and roads and in the many windows. Headlights moved on the expressway. It was all far below.

It feels wrong not to come and wrong to keep coming, she said. But I have to let you go. God, no, I don't mean that. I didn't say that. You're going nowhere. You're not going anywhere, I mean. I mean that you'll get better. You'll be back with us. But not us. We're not us. You're not mine. I do love you. No, I don't mean that. I always will love you, in a way, but not in that way, I don't think. What am I saying? I don't know what I'm saying. Please don't go. Goodnight, Dream-Boy. I know you'll pull out of this.

She thought of a small, falling plane.

A hopeless pilot.

Pull up.

Pull up.

35.

It's a week since the Geologist left. And they're together, doctor and cat. And I'm with them too. I'm here with them, with the cat, with the flat, with the doctor, my doctor. I'm here. I'm the air. The sleeping, breathing air. I'm the tank the fish of her is swimming in. I can know her. I can almost know her, know her movements in my waters. I'm the haunted house her ghost frequents.

The darkening and dimming of the rooms continues. I am darkening. I'm dimming. I am rooms losing shape. And she's hard to keep my focus on, inside me. She's a slippery thought inside my mind. It's true, she's a ghost. I'm haunted. She's a ghost, and growing shadowy and indistinct to me. But I can almost know her. I can almost know her better. I can almost reach her. I can feel her presence, *feel her*, the shape she makes, feel her pressure as she pushes up to standing, her hand on the sofa arm, the soles of her bare feet palming the floor as she moves within me, around me, through me...

Going through me, room to room, hallway to kitchen, she's a feeling. Like my eyes are closed and I'm listening carefully. Like I'm blind. She's a lump in my throat. She's a catch in my chest. She's a shiver on the short hairs at the back of my neck. She's a complicated and fascinating shape parting the air. I hold on to her and hold on to myself. I'm holding myself, and inside me: her. My doctor, asking, *Take a breath for me. A big, deep breath. Hold it.* My doctor, she's a held breath. My doctor, she's listening in the silence of a held breath.

In the kitchen, when she turns the tap, a small part of me adjusts. Water courses and it's me it's travelling through. I'm the squeak of the handle. I'm the neck of the tap, kissed with condensation. I'm the filling glass. I'm the water. I'm the trembling cylinder of water that she's sculpted in her grasp and bears now back into the living room. It's all inside me.

But all of it is she. It's she, creating everything, everything existing around her. Around her, only around her, I exist. I'm the shape she leaves. I'm negative space. I answer these wonderful movements she makes. Here, I form. Here, I separate. It's how I know she's there. It's how I know I'm here. It's what I'm holding on to. It's a thinning thread. And time moves strangely. No one can keep track, not she, not I, not the cat.

When she sleeps, as she now sleeps, I don't know what she's dreaming. What's inside her? I am losing her and losing myself. I hold her within, but my walls are thinning. She can walk through my walls. I can hold her inside, but I can't see inside her. She's the bird in my tree. I can't hear her singing. She's the word in my book. I can't read her. She's the shape of what I loved, preserved in snow.

What's she planning? What's she dreaming? How's this going to go? How much longer can I hold myself together? I can see it all swept up, swept out, sluiced out into the garden – lamps, bowls, CDs, cat food, magazine subscriptions, keys, dried pasta, floorboards, curtains, spiders... and loyalty cards, love letters, bedsheets, photographs... and spilt milk, wine stains, scuffmarks, footsteps, fingerprints...

Breaking me down, breaking us up, cracking me open from within, first the floor then the doors then the ceiling then the walls, so that I creak, crack, buckle, my walls billowing, a beetle carcass deconstructed by ants, broken down to basic ingredients – brick and wood and plaster, blood and bone and dust, busting apart, bursting open, an egg, hatching...

Then, this morning, a letter arrives! We welcome it. An intrusion! I welcome it. Into the flat it slips, into our world, into me, like a splinter under the fingernail. I absorb it. I'm a body absorbing a fragment of bone. It dissolves into me.

She opens the envelope. She reads it in her head then out loud. It's all within me.

He says he thinks he's settling in, she says, parsing for the cat. He says he thinks he could see himself living there… He can't have sent this letter very long after arriving, but he says it suits him. The right amount of *like home* and *not like home*, he says. The snow. The mountains. I can imagine. What else, what else? she says, her eyes moving over the words, lips moving silently before she speaks.

He talks about the landscapes. *They would mean something to anyone. But for me, knowing what I know about the landscapes, about what they are, it's like coming home.* He's a poet! Is that rude of me to say? Rude to someone or other? Keele. Him. Not sure who. But isn't he a poet, when he wants to be, when he's talking about rocks? He sounds well. So, I guess that's it then. He says he won't write again but he wanted to tell someone, and we were the only ones he could think of to tell. Us. You and me. Little old us. He says goodbye, and to say hello to you, Berry.

As she speaks, she's overly animated. I can feel it. Her energy. She's energy, coursing through me. She's synapses, sparking in my brain. As she speaks, the cat looks right at her, sees her, with its unknowing head. Just a clever household mechanism. A vacancy she used to use. A vacancy she used to read her feelings in.

I'm a vacancy, too.

Her feelings move inside me.

Little glimmers in a pond.

So, then, she says, getting up and going to crouch with Berry. I'll pass on to you his best wishes, and she takes the cat's chops in her hands. Then she kisses it square on the muzzle.

Berry licks her nose.

Hello, cat.

Now the animal – the empty creature – stands and leaves the room. But the doctor doesn't follow, for a moment. She stays, crouching. Then, when she does get up, when she does go out into the hallway, she finds that there, in the middle of the hall, in the dead centre of the flat, *there*, round and black like a hole in the floor, offered like the opposite of a gift, there lies Berry where he's chosen that moment to curl himself up in the shape of a fossil and die.

She kneels again. She knows. She does nothing, says nothing. Her hands are on her knees. She's quiet with herself. She touches her brow, lightly. She's feeling the thinness of her own skull. Her skull is a room shapes move around inside. She touches her lips. She's feeling where she kissed the cat's mouth. She places her hand on that sleek back like a black river. She weeps like a silent, black river. She makes no sound. She waits until night.

36.

Ivy waits until night. Ivy, alone. Heard only by herself, she thinks detailed thoughts. There's a rare condition. A defect of the inner ear. She recalls it. She has that doctor's fascination with abnormalities. She has that doctor's ability to retain and call up the name of everything, as if that equates to understanding everything. Unattractive traits, she's sure. But there's this rare condition which she finds herself remembering...

This condition: you can hear your own body. The inside of it. The insides. You hear everything. Every organ. Every bone. Every movement. Each crunch and click. Each quiver and gollop and puff. It's not meant to be that way. Usually there's a trick, a trick the body plays on itself, so you don't hear it. But if you hear it... it tips you overboard. You lose all balance, hearing everything. Your elbow hinging. Your heart beating. The swivel of your eyes in their sockets. Your own voice speaking. It's like hearing the thoughts of every part of you.

And kneeling here, waiting, listening to the stillness, she feels afflicted. She hears every noise in the flat. And more. She hears every noise of the building. Every person. Every room. Every movement. Every sound. It's like the building's her body. It's like a dreadful superpower. Is she afflicted or gifted? She's waiting to bury Berry.

There are Residents' Association rules and written laws about it. She can't bury him in the garden but she buries him in the garden anyway. Long after midnight, she takes a communal spade from the house's stairwell. Not a communal spade. Somebody's spade. Well-kept. Clean. Sharp as a slice of the moon. It's One-Two's spade, of course, so shiny and particular.

Next, going around to that neglected section of flowerbed by her back door, a corner undetected by the motion-sensor light, she shifts stashes of soil for almost an hour. Hearing male laughter, she pauses. Drinkers, in the lane. Someone urinating like a beast. Usually, she's not out here. She could count on one hand the number of times she's hung out in this garden after midnight.

Despite the hard ground, she achieves a too-big grave. Then the body, wrapped in a towel, is put down inside the hole. It's covered over, and the ground stamped down aggressively, so there's no chance of disturbance. She buries it deep, near where they planted a mouse one morning, she and that oversized man she'd let into her life briefly and with whom she'd had nothing in common and about whom she'd had no idea at all.

She feels her head.

Its slenderness. Its brittleness.

Its texture. Its hardness.

Its glossiness. Its gravity.

37.

In the stillness of the flat, she hears every movement of the house: the main door opening and closing, echoey voices in the stairwell, Cox-Coburn walking about on his upper floor, above his lower floor... One-Two at her piano, willing her music to fill the common areas, to fill every other flat, drown out everyone else... the old son, high up in his dead father's rooms, among his dead father's things, taking his father's place in the armchair... and reedy bushes in the garden whispering in the breeze above the muddy ground, above the sleeping bulbs, above Berry's very still body, wrapped in its bath towel, barely beginning to decompose...

Then a new sound seems to enter.

A very small sound. New to the building. Listening, she can see the whole shape of the flat, the whole shape of the house, knowing everything in it, except this new, unusual jingling. A tiny, tinny, Christmassy noise, it's nearby, close, just beyond her room, so light and high, it might actually be inside her, or her imagination. But there it is again.

Shink-a-shink-a-shink.

She lets her arm fall to the floor. She finds her phone where it's charging face down on the carpet. She disconnects it, lifts it, then holds it above her face like she's shielding her eyes on a very sunny day, but it's dark in the room and it's the phone that's as bright as a sun. She switches off the small white aeroplane and a message from Clover arrives.

'Long time, no talk.'

Every so often now, she hears the little bell. Not only in a quiet moment at night but interrupting her throughout the day. She's refilling the cutlery drawer with clattering knives and forks, or changing her whispering shirt, or brush-shush-shushing her teeth when… there it is. Almost there. Almost certainly there. The ghost of a sound, like something at the edge of your vision.

Shinkle-shinkle-shinkle.

Other things, too.

A shadow moving low on the wall in the evening corridor. A swishy tickling around her legs as she hurries, skirted, unbuttoned, half-suited, rushing to dress for work. A familiar feeling she's being observed, watched impassively by something not human.

Then it's in the bounce of sunlight in the swing of the garden gate, as she steps into the lane. It's in that springtime swing of light. It's a sleek, swift creature, white and transparent. It's made of sunlight and breezes. The tinkling of a little collar-bell is in it. There. Not there. Gone. Ghost of a ghost of a ghost.

Or she finds she's sitting with one arm held around herself, the other hand playing at an area of air above her lap, in a daydream, seeming to stroke at the hairs of her own forearm, seeming to stroke at something invisible but substantial, in her lap, in her arms, warm.

Another message from Clover:

'I've met someone! Divorced too.'

'Not that I'm actually divorced! Not actually.'

'I got talking to him. I was phoning you to talk about him. I keep missing you.'

Ivy puts the phone down. She thinks about the Winter Cat, which is what she calls it, that little bell-sound, that sensation of something. Every inch of it is her imagination. She names it Snowdrop. She pictures it. Maybe it's her guardian angel. It might be her angel of death. Most likely, she's mad. She's made it here, to absolute madness. She's arrived here fully in madness. A woman who lives alone.

On her phone again, more messages:

'This man I met, he's an artist!'

'No, I don't know what that means either.'

'How does he make money? That's the question!'

'Handsome.'

'Divorced, too. Like I said. Has a child, too. Tiger's age.'

'That's how we met. His kid is at the same nursery as mine. That's where I was walking when I met him. I was walking through the park when I literally stumbled upon him. Don't ask!'

'He was lying on the ground, you see? In winter! I didn't see him. I tripped right over his feet. He looked like he'd fallen down from the branches, the way he was lying there. I ended up on top of him.'

'An artist, like I say. So, he was being artistic. Lying there. We talked all the way to getting the kids. And I think the kids get on. He's good with kids, of course. He's a father. But so interesting. All these ideas about art. Intense. He reminds me of Iain. He talks about art like Iain talked about poetry.'

'I want to see him again. I'll try, if I can. He's bound to be at the nursery again. Unless it's his wife. His ex, I mean. I think he might be perfect. You'd like him, I know it.'

'So, you see what I'm saying, Ivy? That he's perfect. That he's perfect for you.'

Washing dishes in the kitchen, she sees the animal again, outside. It floats above the wall like a summer heat haze.

Shinkly-shinkly-shinkly-shink… It drips into the garden. It's on the steps. It's at the gate. Stopping. Circling. Against the gate, it puts its hindquarters. It watches Ivy's window.

It seems to be looking right at her. But who knows what cats are ever looking at? It isn't even there, of course, but Ivy watches it watching her, as it backs its haunches against the gate, against the planks, its tail raised like a plume. It's marking its territory. It tenses with the effort, relaxes, then evaporates.

It isn't there, of course, but the next time Ivy leaves for work, she notes the fresh smell of cat urine as she goes into the lane. It's a message. *Keep Out*. But against whom? Against what? Or is it to keep her in?

Messages:

'I get the message. You don't want to talk. But when did you ever? One of us has to, doesn't she? Someone has to start. Maybe you don't think so.'

'About this man, Ivy, this parent at the nursery. I don't know what I was thinking. I got it wrong. I came on too strong. It wasn't like that at all. He wasn't what I thought at all. As good as told me so. He seemed to think I was infatuated! A desperate woman! I seem to have made a fool of myself again. Oh, well. Onward and upward.'

'What about you, Sis? Have I made a fool of myself with you, too?'

'I think you misunderstood me about Iain. I didn't

mean what you think. It wasn't anything. Not my place to feel anything more than you. It's yours. It's nothing. I think you think I said I loved him or something. I was getting carried away. It was only to be close to you.'

'I'm not divorcing either, by the way. That wasn't anything, either. It's nothing. We have Tiger. We're a family. That means something. Don't say it doesn't. I want it. I want my family. It isn't perfect but it's family. I know you won't but please don't say anything to Him Indoors.'

'Well. Onward.'

'Upward.'

'Maybe I am a fool, but I don't mind as long as you talk to me.'

38.

It was an early autumn afternoon and, when she went to investigate those odd little noises outside her door, out of the blue a black cat was there. It skipped immediately between her legs and into her kitchen. An hour was wasted chasing it around the rooms, with no small number of knocked-over items. It was adept at evading her. But when she finally gave up and sat down, it came over. It started sniffing at her and studying her edges until it got itself onto her lap.

Well, how could I kick you out now, cat?

Yesterday evening, she had said goodbye to Keele. Now she stroked this new visitor, wondering how it had come to be that she'd never kept another cat since Nana died. Probably it had been because of Keele not wanting one. Probably it had been Keele's apathy about cats. Funny, given how apathetic cats are about people!

Later, when the little black cat still hadn't gone, Ivy

cooked fishfingers for it and ate one herself. That night, she left the back door open. What was she thinking?! You'd only do that in this city if you were a dimwit or a hardcase or had a naïve belief in the virtuousness of humankind. But the cat had to know it could leave if it wished.

It had no collar. She took a photo and printed off copies. Grayscale. No need for colour. The cat was black except for a white smudge behind the ear. Ivy went around the neighbourhood, sticking up posters, taping them to streetlamps, stapling them to trees.

Lost Cat? Call: …

Over the next few days, three people did call. They said they'd spotted it, her lost cat, hanging around on nearby streets. When they'd approached, it was unbelievably nifty. A daredevil. Acrobatic and perilous. It seemed the animal had been cropping up a lot, all over the neighbourhood. Appearing, disappearing.

'When did you lose it?' they asked her.

No, she told them. I've *found* a cat, not lost one.

A fourth person phoned. A murkier, craftier voice than the others, somehow seeming to come from the dark, from shadows. 'I caught him. Your pet. It took some doing, but I have him. Dead or alive, right? Heh heh. The wanted poster said that, didn't it? Heh heh. No, not a scratch on him. Don't worry. Hardly a scratch on him. Can't say the same of myself, but that's another story… Now, in all seriousness, let's talk rewards…'

She put out new posters – *Cat Found* – and no one else called.

The cat stayed. Until someone phoned, Ivy took care of it. No one phoned. By the end of the week, she'd been shopping. The flat was supplied with the correct, nutritional food and a book on feline care. Recklessly, she'd had a cat-flap installed. But her little guest didn't go near it.

Then it did leave. But it returned within the hour, and for much of the time it was outside Ivy watched from the kitchen window, checking that it didn't go far. It didn't go far. A cautious cat. A cautious woman. She'd watched, waiting for its return, while it crept around the garden, sniffing at flowerpots and corners, taking fright at insects and far-off sounds. It was a nervous animal. Each paw seemed constructed with its own little spring. The feet were always skipping and boinging erratically.

I know how you feel, Ivy said, when the cat came back inside, exhausted.

Unusually perhaps, Ivy was chatty, cheery. She was falling very naturally into the routines of this new friendship.

So, what are tonight's plans? Shall we go out? No, okay, another night in.

The cat was on her lap when the phone rang. One hand held the phone and the other she held out slackly so the cat's little paws could play slapsies with her as she listened.

It was Lee.

My Iain. Our boy.

'I already knew,' Lee said. 'I knew a week ago. He was there. But something had changed. Did you notice? He was there but not there. He was fading in and out. Then he really was gone. Did you see it? Whatever it was, it had left him. He wasn't there anymore. I knew I had to let him go. Then his body packed up. The doctors took over the decision-making. I held his hand. But his hand was something else. It wasn't his. It was out of place. From another world. It didn't feel like a hand at all.'

Listening, Ivy stroked at the cat, somewhat robotically. She couldn't listen too closely. It hurt to listen too closely. You had to maintain a professional distance. She was rubbing at the pads of the cat's paws. They were exceptionally soft, pink pads for a stray.

What are you, little black cat? Ivy thought. *Are you royalty? Look at these pads! You've never worked a day in your life, have you?*

Meanwhile, in Ivy's ear, Lee described her own grief. Were they sharing in something? Was Ivy's grief meant to listen now, as Lee's grief spoke? Lee seemed able to speak it all. It seemed good for her, speaking it. Was this where Keele had got it from, all those words pouring like wine? The grief, Lee elaborated, was a creature. Her grief was a creature that had followed her home from the hospital. It was like that, like an attendant animal. It was hers now.

She didn't have him but she had this new thing – her grief – which was almost like a living thing.

She'd invited it in, she said. She knew she had. Maybe that wasn't advised, but she hadn't thought twice. Was it denial or acceptance? She didn't know. It hardly mattered. It would live with her now for a number of years, this creature. For how many years, who knew? Could you outlive it? Could it outlive you? It was hers. It was hers, and in her custody it would need caring for, feeding, accommodating – this aloof, charismatic, enigmatic animal. It would always be with her now, distant and self-interested but always there, insatiable and demanding and there no matter how she felt about it; there, and nothing she could do about it.

Ivy was quiet. Ivy didn't know. She was sure Lee was right, but she didn't know. She was sure Lee was right, but how did Lee know all that already? How did she have so many words for it? For Ivy, it was simply happening to her. How was Lee so literate in something so unknowable and uncontainable? How come she knew what the creature was? Listening, Ivy tickled Berry's chin and imagined the beast at her door.

'What choice is there?' Lee was saying. 'Shutting the door is no choice at all. That's not living. All you can say is, "Welcome! Wipe your claws on the mat! Come on in!"'

39.

Coming through the gate, coming into the garden, another nightshift, another morning finding her way home, drunk on overwork, she discovers the man waiting for her. He isn't wearing his hat, but she recognizes him. She knows him by the hat he isn't wearing. A head that ought to have a hat. But she sees him more clearly, too, with the hat off. She sees all those features in him now. The cragginess. The generous nose. The brows like outcrops. The weathered skin. It's the same face! A thinner version, but it's the same face.

She says hello and continues past him along the path, towards her door, as if he's nothing to do with her (which he isn't), as if he's just another neighbour and she doesn't really know who he is, what he is.

'Miss, a moment of your time,' he says.

She turns back, smiling blankly. He's holding his hat in both hands. He's taken it off out of old-fashioned politeness, she supposes. Now he replaces it on his head. He puts in a lot of attention and effort arranging it there. The face changes.

He says, 'You're wondering who I am and what I'm doing outside your flat.'

No, she says. She isn't wondering. She knows who he is. She likes the power of knowing, likes letting him know that she knows. She holds it a little longer. Then she tells him who he is. He's Grant's brother. The Geologist's brother.

'Knox,' he says. 'Grant's brother, Knox.'

If you're looking for Grant, I can't help you.

'Told you about me, has he?'

She doesn't answer.

'Not like him to tell anyone anything, but I can see he's told you about me.'

He hasn't. Not really. But she put it together somehow. She never knew much about Grant, all said and done, but somehow she's seen it: these two faces. Brothers. The man in a hat and the Geologist. No, Grant said very little about his family, but she knows he has a brother. She's gathered that. And if he said nothing, wasn't that saying something? She says nothing now. She waits. She'll be like Grant. She'll be a stone. She'll give nothing away.

'I don't blame him if he doesn't want to see me,' says this man, Knox. 'But we're brothers. I don't mean to be bad for him. The way we were raised. The way Dad was.

How else can I be? The way we were raised. What other way was I going to turn out? How Grant turned out? Could have gone two ways, maybe. Two choices. Rise above it or be brought down by it. I went one way. Grant went the other. We can't all be good. We can't all be like Grant. I guess it was the making of him. I guess it made me, too…

'Look, Miss Dover,' he says, moving closer. 'Yes, I know you, Miss Dover. Doctor Dover. Ivy. I know you. I know you know him. I've asked around. I want him. To get a hold of him. Look, I know I'm no good. I'm not a good man. But we're brothers. You know how it is with brothers. Doesn't mean we don't love each other. It isn't all on me. You know how he is. You must have seen it. He's got a way, hasn't he? Keeps you wondering. Let's you play yourself out. Enough rope to hang yourself. A sly bastard, he can be. Do you disagree? You think he's genuine? You're so sure he's good, all the way down?'

He keeps pulling back, trying to compose himself, trying to keep his hands in check.

'I'm not saying I haven't got a temper. I've got a temper. There, I've a said it. A temper. First to admit it. First to throw a punch. I'm a fighter and I've had to be. The way I was raised. But isn't he partly to blame, standing there, saying nothing, saying everything with all his saying nothing, doing me down, doing Dad down? Better than us, is he? Always taking no part. Always upping sticks.

Brothers shouldn't be always disappearing on each other. Makes you angry. Why wouldn't it? Makes you feel like shit, all right? It hurts, someone wanting nothing to do with you. Aye, I lash out. I've thrown a punch or two. Worse. But did he really never do anything to me? Is it really doing nothing? Is it really nothing to someone, if you have nothing to do with them?'

Ivy speaks now. She shouldn't. Or should she? What choice does she have? She's afraid. The way Knox moves and talks. She's afraid. He might take a swing at her if she goes on saying nothing. *But don't say too much, Ivy. Hold back. Hold back.*

He's even closer. He's ever closer. He's turned with her, as she's moved towards the door. She's almost pressed against the door, keys in hand. She's keeping the keys hidden in her fist. The teeth of the keys bite into the squeeze of her fingers. It feels like he's backed her up against her door. She is, she's backed against the door. The teeth of the keys in her fist. *Fight or flight? Fight. Flight.*

She speaks. I don't know, she says. I don't know much about it. I really can't say that I know him that well. Only to say hi to. But… she says. But… isn't it better to let someone be? If that's what they want? Shouldn't we do what's best for other people? Even if it isn't what they want, isn't it better, if it's what's best for them, if you just know that's the best thing for them?

'Listen,' he says. 'Ivy. Hold on. Listen. Let's talk.' He's reached out. He has a hand planted flat against her door. 'Let's go in. Let me come in. Just to talk. What are you looking like that for? What are you looking so afraid of? You're holding out on me, I can tell. I could tell it before, at the hospital, too. You know more than you're letting on. Thinking you know best. Thinking you're better. Just like Grant. Sly. Withholding. Make you feel good? All about what you need, is it? What about me? What about what I need? In on it together, you two. Thick as fucking thieves.'

Please, she says. Knox. My wrist. You're hurting me.

'He never even knew Mum. I did. Dad did. It isn't like he thinks. He never even knew her. He's so sure she was a saint, is he? Still holding on to that bit of nonsense? He should let that go. His dad's dead. Does that make a difference? Does he still want nothing to do with us, even if he's dead? Hates him that much, even dead? Hates us that much?'

Knox's hat has tipped up. It's come off.

'Must have told you it was me, did he? His head. Doctor's orders, to reveal all? You his priest now, are you? Told you it was me? That's his version. That's his story. What about my side? It's easy to leave, Ivy. Easy to have nothing to do with it. Someone had to stay with that arsehole, that devil. Is it my fault if I'm my father's son? Is it all on me? Who else's son would I be? Who says he can have nothing to do with me? Who says you can just move on? I'm his brother. This is love. Love, yes, I can say love. This is what love looks like. Look, let's go in. Let's talk. Just let me in a moment…'

My arm. Let go.

He doesn't. He hasn't. She's pressed against the door. He might strike her down. He might beat the door down. She didn't realize Knox's size before. The weight and power. Like Grant. Is this what frightened her in Grant? And Knox is drunk, she realizes. Knox was always drunk. In the hospital, too, when he came looking for Grant. A simmer of drunkenness. And she's at his mercy. She's uselessly weak. It's dreadful, being a woman, submitting to this. If she was a man. If she was Grant. Iain Keele.

'Wait,' says Knox. 'Hold on. Just hold on.'

Crack.

He's stumbled back. Hit once. And the neighbour's spade sways. It's the spade from the stairwell, the spade Ivy used for digging Berry's hole. It swings again.

One.

Two.

And Knox is bleeding from his mouth.

'Out!' says One-Two, still gripping the spade near the blade. She's hit him hard. She hit him with the handle, not the blade. One-Two doesn't want a murder on her hands. What would the neighbours think? But she hit him hard.

'Out! Get out of here!'

She's jabs towards him. She eyeballs him.

'I know you,' she says. 'I know your type. No business here. Look where you are. Private land, this garden. Look around you. What are you doing here? This is a doctor you're accosting. A doctor! One of the professions. What are you? Look at yourself. Do you even work? You don't belong here. Belong in the gutter. Out!'

She brandishes the handle at him. Ivy watches One-Two, powerlessly.

Knox is bent forwards, doubled over. For a second, Ivy's worried that he'll grab the spade from her. But he's moved away, backwards, into the garden. He touches his mouth, mashes his lips.

'No cause,' he says, muzzily.

He's looking always at Ivy.

'No cause. That wasn't me. I'm leaving. But I didn't do any of this. I'm leaving, but don't say you didn't bring it on yourself.'

'Leave then, if you're leaving,' says One-Two. She swings the spade like she's in a parade.

'Leave! I know your type. No, I know *you*! I *know* you. You came to the flat. You spoke to my lodger. The fight. You! I thought you'd bring the whole building down. Get out of here. Find your rock to crawl under. Must be pubs opening soon. Must be a bar hasn't barred you. Leave. Leave now. One of you was bad enough. One of you was more than enough.'

He's found his hat again. He replaces it, like it matters. His face is blank, under the hat. The mouth is cut and bloody.

'Well, I'm leaving,' he says. 'Anyway, I'm leaving. I won't be the problem. I won't hang around being anyone's excuse. I'll be gone. Then he'll see.'

They watch him walking up the steps and through the gate into the lane then heading towards the road, moving along the other side of the wall. The hat travels along the top of the wall. They carry on standing their ground. They tremble.

One-Two pushes the spade into the lawn so it stands upright without her but she doesn't let go. Then after a while, she goes inside, makes tea and brings it out to them. It takes time. They're calmer.

'No thanks is necessary,' says One-Two. 'Among us, no one owes anyone. Owners owe nothing. We have to stick together, the owners. For the house. Members only.'

40.

After One-Two's gone indoors, Ivy stays outside longer. It's morning, but what time is it? People have been leaving for work. The tea is cold. She sits on the doorstep and means to go inside soon. She wonders who'll be next through the gate.

All around her, the garden is dormant. But soon the crocuses will come nosing up from the earth, sticking squat snouts out of the grass and mud to crouch like little frogs of many colours. Then the cherry park will fill with pink snow. An avalanche of blossom.

She looks at the flowerbed beside her. The heavily patted-down earth.

'I noticed the gardening you've been doing,' One-Two had said, before she'd gone indoors. 'You're really putting down roots, Ivy. What was it? Bulbs, is it? Planted good and deep, haven't you? You're sure it'll find its way out?'

It's quiet. Ivy's alone, perching on her own doorstep. Grant is a long time ago. Keele is a long time ago. Berry's in the ground at her feet. But Ivy's going nowhere. If she sits still enough, she can watch spring arrive. She can watch her life changing. It's what she'll do. Be still. Stop. Sit. Settle. Stay. A woman who lives alone, she'll own it.

Coming from the lane then, she hears it; but is it the same bell?

Slink-slink-slink.

Then she sees the neighbour cat clear the wall. Gold. In a single bound, it seems. Golden. Almost like it's stepping over the whole wall on those long, golden, stork-like legs. It comes to her. It stops beside her. It makes no sound, won't look at her. It is frank and cool and judgemental. It sits back, settles, stays, sitting high on its front legs. There, at her side, it stays.

Its tall neck reaches to a flat yellow head. Ivy places a hand there. It allows her. She's a queen laying a hand on the arm of a throne. They watch the garden. After some time, of its own accord, the neighbour cat leaves and may come back some day.

Then here's the postwoman she knows by name, weaving through her village-city. Morning, morning. Into Ivy's hand she places a letter like an unpeeled fruit. A deep blue stamp bearing a horned creature, a finned creature, a knotted rope, a boat, a moon... It's come from some-where cold and faraway. Thank you! Goodbye!

And Ivy stands and finally unlocks her door.
She should locate the landline. She should ring Clover.
She goes in.
Hello, flat, she calls. Did you miss me?

Acknowledgements

Thanks to my wife and the girls. Thanks, Mum. Enormous thanks both to my agent Cara Lee Simpson at Peters Fraser + Dunlop and to my editor Kate Ballard at Atlantic Books for understanding so clear-sightedly what the book was and helping it to be more fully itself, which (just like for Ivy, Berry and Grant) is all it ever really wanted. Thank you to the whole team at Atlantic Books and to my copyeditor, Belinda Jones. Thanks to my readers: Aga, Catherine, Jenni, Micaela and Salka. All my love to Chris and Franki. Finally, thanks to all the cats – *you know who you are.*